ZENOBIA

Writings from an Unbound Europe

■ □ ■ □ ■

GELLU NAUM

ZENOBIA

Translated by James Brook and Sasha Vlad

NORTHWESTERN UNIVERSITY PRESS

EVANSTON, ILLINOIS

Northwestern University Press
Evanston, Illinois 60208-4210

Printed in the United States of America

ISBN CLOTH 0-8101-1254-X
ISBN PAPER 0-8101-1255-8

And all of us who were alive thought we were dead
and walked about in a daze . . .

Ioan Dobrescu, furrier in the Bateşti Quarter of Bucharest, October 1813

■ □ ■ □ ■

CONTENTS

■ □ ■ □ ■

ACKNOWLEDGMENTS

The translators wish to thank Oana Lungescu and Zack Rogow for their invaluable corrections, comments, and encouragement on the antepenultimate draft of this book; this translation also benefited from the kindness of Luba Jurgenson and Sebastian Reichmann, who made available their French translation of *Zenobia*.

I

■ □ ■ □ ■

THE SWAMPS

1. TOO MANY THINGS SOLICIT US, AND, GIVEN THE EQUIVOCAL solicitation mechanism, too many words flock to contain them, to hide them in their useless and deceiving labyrinth —that's why I might sometimes tell you what shouldn't be told; anyway, I am convinced that everyone will meditate more on the surplus, leaving aside the state in which I float, below, like a frogman, for instance.

But there is also that rumble and everyone's capacity to perceive it . . .

2. So it was a July morning—an unusually chilly one, now that I think of it; it had been raining monotonously and monstrously all night long, the sky still looked like a purplish sponge soaked in water; I was soaked to the bone, but what bothered me most was the mud that seeped through the holes in my rubber boots and made a cold and slippery mess all over my cotton socks.

I had been standing for several hours, covered in mud from head to toe, and, as I was saying, soaked through, stuck in a crack in the dam, a crevasse, listening to its breathing and its groans; certainly, it was all the same to me and, at the edge of the forest, where I later tried to take refuge under the trees, in the bushes, I heard so much calm, indifferent rustling mixed in with the void of silence, that I felt as if I were enclosed in a giant drop of water that was

THE SWAMPS

I
▼

thinking and breathing for us, like that, as in the beginning; but don't worry, I'll soon be in a dry room, in a warm place somewhere, among the soothing, indifferent noises of people and objects, all of which will think and breathe for me.

Nearby, on the left bank of the swamp, stood Mr. Sima's ivy-covered house: I knew him vaguely; some sort of retired person, he was interested in the virtues of medicinal plants, I often met him in the fields, he gathered blue flowers, we even greeted each other, that's why I knocked at his door—I saw how drops ran from my fist and not from the wood of the wet door—and I shouted: "Open up!"

He opened the door—he was dry—with a friendly smile and asked me to come in; the coating of water remained outside—I mean, that drop that extends over the world and contains it—we went deeper into its interior, forgetting it, as usual, opened one door, then another, Mr. Sima wanted to give me some dry rags, so I could change my clothes, you know, people help one another; I declined, it was good, it was warm, Mr. Sima said, "Let's go upstairs, there are some more people there, let's at least have a cup of tea together—"

"What *people*, Mr. Sima? Do you think I care about *people* right now? I'm dog tired, I can hardly stand, I could lie down over here, on the floor, can't you hear how I rustle?"

"The tea will do you good, Mr. Naum. It's an herb tea, it's good for you."

"Well, if you insist," and so on, until we reached the upstairs room, I won't describe it, I will only say that there were four more people, two young men and a girl whom, naturally, I loved at first sight, and, on a long table made of thick planks and placed under the window overlooking the swamps, there was another, older man, stretched out, it seemed that he was either sleeping or dead or a wax dummy. His face looked familiar, but I didn't know from where. When I walked in, he opened his eyes and looked at me for an instant, then closed them again and didn't move anymore.

"This is Mr. Naum, he's a distinguished poet, I'm sure you've heard of him," was how Mr. Sima deemed it necessary to introduce me.

"Naum to whom?" asked one of the young men, I won't describe him, I'll only say that he was short and thickset and that he had womanly breasts and his curly hair met in two points above his forehead.

"Naum Fu Kyu," I answered him in my mind, because I had to become vulgar, because I loved that girl madly, and I felt, despite myself, sublime, so something had to be done about it, and vulgarity—sacrilege—generally counterbalances sublimity, on occasion; but I answered like that only in my mind because I didn't want to counterbalance that young man; and I added aloud: "You can call me whatever you want, it doesn't matter."

"Then I will call you 'Constantinescu,'" he declared.

It was all the same to me, I was looking at that girl, my eyes had lit up with happiness, I loved her madly, and in my mind I was saying to her: "Oh, I love you so unimaginably much!"

Mr. Sima poured us tea, it was sweet-smelling and minty, anyway, I won't describe it, I will only say that the four of us sat down on chairs—there were four chairs in the room—and that young man with the womanly breasts, who, as I found out later, was called Jason (he held the teacup in his left hand), settled on top of the dead man or wax dummy stretched out over there, it seemed that Jason didn't see him.

"It's all right," Mr. Sima said to me in an undertone when I was about to draw Jason's attention to the fact that it's not nice to sit on someone who opens his eyes and looks at you with such an expressive gaze, even if he is dead, even if he is a wax dummy, "it's all right, Dragoş can stand it, it hurts him, but he can take it, he who saw so many things in his time" (so, that one stretched out on the table was called Dragoş); "you'd better say something to the girl who is looking at you as if you were her long-awaited bridegroom."

"My dear," I said then, softly, to that girl, "because I don't know your name I will call you Zenobia, and you should know that I love you so unimaginably much; look, just last night I dreamed that a friend of mine, a former schoolmate, I don't remember exactly, gave me an embroidered coat, I had to attend his wedding; well, the bride, who looked exactly like you, loved me so unimaginably much, she was always telling me that in spite of my reserved attitude, I admit that it was pleasant, although I firmly rebuffed her passionate tendencies; besides, a few nights before, in almost the same situation (except for the nuptial ceremony) another girl, not a bride but one who was known to be a Mormon, please do not overlook this detail, also loved me so unimaginably much, and I was feeling so very good, like in that drop of water; I was happy in her film of love, I'm telling you the truth, and I love you so unimaginably much, and so on; this state of love for you, total and encompassing, sums up my whole existence until now, I don't know whether you understand me; and if you too love me so unimaginably much, as it seems that you do, you can ignore my physical person which is so incorrectly dressed, it doesn't matter, I don't know whether you understand me, and I'm asking you to forgive this idiotic speech, I meant to say, and so on—"

"Certainly I love you," she answered in a low voice, "besides, you should know that, circumstances aside, I love you so unimaginably much, as your former schoolmate's bride, even though I'm not a Mormon, but that doesn't matter, and so on—"

"Hey, Constantinescu," Jason said aloud, "what are you two mumbling about, why are you even looking at that wretch? She's scum, I found her in the swamps, almost unconscious; while we were coming here, I kicked her several times to teach her a lesson, I would have left her there to die in the water, in the reeds, but Petru took her along, out of pity" (so, the other, much younger one, almost a child, was called Petru), "and he brought her here."

"I didn't bring her out of pity," said Petru, "but because I love her so unimaginably much, although I don't even know her name."

"Her name is Zenobia, if you don't mind," I said, "and she's unimaginably beautiful, even in this state and almost unconscious, like when you brought her here from the swamps; I've known her for a long time, before my former schoolmate's wedding, and so on—"

"I don't care what her name is," said Petru, "her name could just as well be Zenobia, if she chooses; I fell for her so unimaginably much at first sight and I don't give a damn about her name or her marriages."

Because Petru got carried away with talking—maybe the mint tea was starting to have its effect on us too—Jason began to laugh; and to be able to do that more easily he jumped up on the table, perhaps intentionally, and onto the stomach of that dead man or dummy who opened his eyes and looked desperately at Mr. Sima.

3. As I write, because it seems that I am writing, I regret that you don't have in front of you the sheets of paper on which these lines of ink are crammed; if you did have them, if you closed your eyes and lightly passed your fingertips over this rain of black letters, I'm sure that you would *see* Mr. Sima's room with the table under the window overlooking the swamps, with its dead man and all; and you would see us, each in his place, talking to himself or out loud; and you would understand that nothing of the states so far is imagined, that everything happened exactly as I am narrating it. Once you're here, I would advise you to stop a moment and review, with your eyes closed, passing your ten fingertips lightly over the pages; unburdened by words, inside the film of your own receptiveness, perhaps you will discover the extremely important things that, as much as I might wish to, are impossible for me to convey.

I would advise you then to practice this reviewing exercise whenever you doubt the truthfulness of my account; as for me, given where I am right now, it doesn't matter; you might be offered the chance to enter the place where you only think that you are, and so on . . .

4. Thinking that it was time to intervene and put an end to a situation that threatened to become ever more unbearable, Mr. Sima turned to the dead man or dummy stretched out on the table under the window overlooking the swamps and said to him in a low voice: "Don't worry, Dragoş, I will do everything possible to save you."

Then he spoke aloud to Jason: "Young man, I ask you to show some respect for the house you are in and stop sitting on the table; moreover, I ask you to finally stop that abject and absolutely out-of-place laughter of yours. All the people here are my guests, and I won't ever permit anyone to laugh at them in my presence."

"Take it easy," answered Jason, getting off the table, to the obvious relief of Dragoş, who smiled, "don't take it like that, we're only human, and why shouldn't I laugh at these sorry cases, just take a look at them, take a look at Constantinescu, and at Petru, and at this bitch," and Jason emphasized his last words with a well-aimed boot at Zenobia's slender waist; Petru and I gasped, as if we ourselves felt the kick, the otherwise rather reserved Mr. Sima sketched a gesture of indignation, only Dragoş smiled, now indifferent: "I can't help laughing, just take a look at them!"—and wham! he kicked Zenobia again with his boot—"you'd laugh just at the sight of them, poor devils—" And wham! he kicked me, too, with his boot—

Certainly, and please remember this detail, anyone would have expected something to intervene and stop the rude unleashing of Jason's brutality; there was a well-sharpened ax hanging on a pole, any one of us could easily have split his head open with it; or Mr. Sima, who had a rifle in the room downstairs, I had seen it, could have run and gotten it, and bang! he could have snuffed Jason for good, we would have helped him afterward to throw Jason over Dragoş and out the window, into the swamps, he could count on our silence and complicity; or Petru could have invoked their ties of friendship, their years spent together in school, and so on; or Zenobia, oh, if she had wanted to, could have at least shouted; or Dragoş, well, no, Dragoş was perhaps dead, so he couldn't do anything, and I, who was more powerful . . .

5. Once, in the field, above the dam that was newly reinforced after the floods, there was a menacing sky, sparrows and weeds tried to scratch my eyes, nobody loved me, I was in a circle of unrestrained hostility, in that deserted place, and the wind was whistling past my ears, actually one ear, the left one, was aching, I was in need of someone, badly in need of escaping, of getting out of the circle, I was in need of someone who would love me at least until the danger had passed, when I noticed that earthen boulder, it was ugly, black, repulsive; of course, the boulder brought down upon itself all the curses, all the sky's hostility, it loved me, it crouched, turned even blacker, and burst, seemingly tense and bearing all agony, for me, for the whole world, for the whole endangered planet; then the sparrows minded their own business, they became friendly again, the weeds rustled as pleasantly as possible, a great burden was lifted from my soul, but now there was nobody . . .

6. So because Jason represented, in my eyes, the substance of another circle and I had no intention of absorbing his hostility, I said in a loud, almost declamatory voice: "We all live and squirm inside the same fragile film; look, for instance, if Jason agreed, if Petru agreed, and if Mr. Sima approved, because it seems to me that the rain has stopped, I would leave with Zenobia, whom I love so unimaginably much; I would go with her, I mean, to the end of the world, I mean,

no, to somewhere closer, to places that I know; in this way the circle menacing us right now could break, and we could squirm together or separately, among black boulders, and you, Jason, you could go to hell!"

At this point, my eyes glanced at the ax, and I was about to rush to it but I refrained because Zenobia, understanding me quite well, crouched on the floor and started to absorb.

Certainly, Mr. Sima quickly agreed to our departure, the rain had stopped completely, Zenobia, crouched on the floor, started to blacken and even to burst, it seemed, here and there, beneath the sheet of plastic that covered her, and I, looking at Jason, who thought this the best moment to comb his hair with a little yellowish comb made of bone, felt growing inside me the desire to crack his head open with the ax, when Petru, quiet and pale, said: "Of course, Mr. Sima quickly agreed to your departure, Jason is combing his hair, Zenobia is crouching and blackened, she has to fight more overwhelming forces, but I, Petru, quiet and pale, I love her, and what will become of me? I will squirm alone, I will wander the face of the earth like a coffin, carrying inside me an almost unconscious image of her, whom I love so unimaginably much, I will talk to her, in my mind, in forests, and railroad stations, I will make her bed inside me and put her to sleep every night, I will wrap her in rags, you know very well how many rags each of us is carrying inside himself and how many people sleep wrapped in them, inside each of us, and she will never answer me because she won't hear me when I sing her a lullaby, because there, inside me, she will wrap her own lover in the rags inside her, he in turn will carry her in the rags inside him, and he will rock her and sing her a lullaby, and so on; and I will go alone, quiet and pale, and you will take me into yourselves, never mind, it was meant to be that way . . ."

After his long speech, young Petru fell silent, then he

opened the door and went down the stairs, while the rest of us, except Jason who continued to comb his hair, went to the window and looked out over Dragoş, Zenobia got up from the floor and came over beside me, even Dragoş, moved by a sudden curiosity, looked outside over his own body; and we saw for the last time the one who had left our company, advancing farther into the swamps, carrying himself, quiet and pale, in his own arms, like a coffin . . .

"Here," he shouted to us, pointing to his heart with his finger, "here is Zenobia, *à jamais,* and here is where I will put you to sleep and wrap you up, every night . . ."

Then he disappeared among the swaying reeds, and Zenobia touched my shoulder with her shoulder wrapped in that dirty sheet of plastic, unpleasant to the touch, the rags were inside, I felt good wrapped in them, and we left together, shoulder to shoulder, without even looking at Jason.

Certainly, before leaving we thanked Mr. Sima for his hospitality and even waved a brief farewell to Dragoş, who, opening his eyes for an instant, gave us an unimaginably friendly smile.

7. I took Zenobia to the hollow of the dam, and we squirmed there for I don't know how long, without saying a word, lying shoulder to shoulder, with our faces pressed against the wet dirt of that alveolus; it was a great love, and we clutched each other in the darkness, and beyond us was the film that contains us all, like an amoeba hidden in each of us.

After a while, I went with Zenobia to the forest—we never parted, please remember this detail, even if it sometimes looks otherwise to you—to listen to the rustling of the bushes and to get news of the world; this happened under the sign of the Old Lovers, and we saw them floating above us, the two old giants who, toward fall, cover the sky; as they passed, the forest filled with moans and mumbling, you would swear it was thundering; then they were gone: we thanked them for the news, and off we went, shoulder to shoulder, into the field.

After a while, we realized that the splendid fall that covered the world was nearing its end; and since winters are especially harsh in the swamps, we prepared for hibernation; with our own hands we enlarged the hollow, we lined it with branches that offered themselves to us, we left only a door and a little window covered with woven twigs, so we could open them if need be, we scattered half-wilted wildflowers on the floor, we dug a well inside and, of course, a little latrine; the days passed slowly, the sun turned more and more orange.

8. Now that we're here, please review, while I, waiting for winter, would read aloud for hours at a time, and Zenobia would accompany me by beating, with only two fingers, a little drum made out of a piece of leather found in the water, dried in the wind, and stretched across a hollow log; her strange rhythms reminded me of the sounds of cranes preparing to head south.

I knew nothing of the others, maybe Petru was still wandering across the swamps (the last reed of the north said that it saw him going by on his way to the city); as for Jason, I, still offended by his behavior during our brief encounter, wanted to forget him.

From time to time, on our rare outings away from the hollow, Zenobia and I ran in the field to stretch our limbs; that is, I ran, because she flew, attached to my shoulder.

Once, when we stopped to catch our breath on a knoll, I saw from afar Mr. Sima and Dragoş, they were picking, apparently, the last of the blue flowers; we greeted them from a distance, I waved my right arm, Zenobia waved her left arm because my left shoulder was attached to her right shoulder; Mr. Sima and Dragoş responded with friendly gestures made with whatever arm they chose, because they weren't attached shoulder to shoulder.

9. We went on living like this for weeks, like moles, in our shelter, and the immense sky stretched out high above us; at night, it adorned itself with all its stars, unfolding endlessly; Zenobia was continuing her whispers, she talked with my shoulders, with my mouth, with my knees—during that time, I very seldom heard her speak directly to me, as if to an entity, except at the moments when she was telling me that she loved me so unimaginably much, that she had loved me even before we met; the winter had come, a harsh winter, with blizzards and lots of snow, the dirt and the dried branches in our hollow rustled faintly, the water in the well hardly rippled when we brought our trembling lips to its surface, we heard only, from time to time, a yell outside, the blizzard perhaps, and so on, then I would be startled and shout "Who's there?" and nobody would answer, but one time someone answered.

"It is I—Mr. Sima."

"Mr. Sima? Look who's here, what a surprise!" and I rushed to the window but didn't open it. "Well! You were the last person I expected! What brings you here?"

"I looked and looked for you," he said. "I feared that the wolves that crossed the Danube to these places had eaten you; yesterday I saw a calf running like mad, blood waving like a mane, wolves had bitten its neck, I never go out without my rifle."

"Well, of course, it's easy for you, you have that rifle from the room downstairs," I said to him, "whereas we, that is, Zenobia and I, buried here like moles, don't have anything, we make love and that's all; I'm sorry that I can't invite you inside, Mr. Sima, there isn't enough room, but tell me the truth, what made you come here in such a blizzard?"

"Well, you see, I brought you some herbs, they contain vitamins, they're for you to keep, just in case, they're good, open the door so I can give them to you."

"You're probably a wolf, Mr. Sima, and you want me to open up so you can shoot us with that rifle and eat us afterward; why don't you come closer while I open the window, to make certain that it's you, to convince myself."

I opened the window, Mr. Sima came closer, I stretched out my arm, I felt his face, my fingers froze, it was him all right, I saw him clearly, he was crying.

"Come on, Mr. Sima, you're a grown-up, be a man, stop crying," I said.

Mr. Sima tottered, buffeted by the gusting wind.

"You're a happy man," he sighed, "it's easy for you to talk like that, because she's protecting you."

"It seems to me that you're becoming delirious, because of the cold, Mr. Sima; I live here, don't ask me under what conditions, and you say that she's protecting me. Who's protecting me? You don't mean Zenobia, by any chance?"

"You know very well who," he said.

"What else can I say, Mr. Sima?" I asked. "Everyone conveys his errors the best he can, and they always contain a bit of truth; the others understand as much as they can; everyone tells less than he understands and understands more than he is told, and what he understands is not told, because what is told he doesn't understand, and so on. But let's forget about those stupid things, let's be reasonable, Mr. Sima; come on, tell me, what's the matter, why are you crying?"

Mr. Sima removed, with his right thumb and index finger—he held his rifle in his left hand—a big tear that had frozen in the corner of his eye, and dropped it; the falling tear made a tiny hole in the snow, barely visible, like a needle prick, and that was all; then he said: "What's the matter is that I'm going to die soon, I don't think I'll live until spring."

"Be serious, Mr. Sima," I said, "you look healthy as a horse, you should chase away *these dark thoughts*."

"You know very well that things are exactly as I say, and I'm crying because that is the custom on such occasions," Mr. Sima replied. "Besides, I took care of everything, I left the house and everything else to a relative, some distant cousin or other, a magistrate in the Bacău district, he will come to bury me; I saved Zenobia a dress from who-knows-what great-grandmother, I found it in the attic, in a chest, it's rotten but still holds together; for you I brought some blue trousers, they're patched a little but they're still good, a shirt with ruffles, a pair of white boots, I think they were for skating, they don't have skates now, I couldn't find any other kind, and some other things, a pair of socks, I don't know what else, a fur cap, I'll bring them over when I come again, maybe you'll go to the city, you have to wear more decent clothes, the way you look won't do; but let's skip these trifles, let's think about Dragoş, because I will be leaving him with you, my relative would be capable of not seeing him and throwing him in the garbage; I'll bring him here, table and all, he will help me carry the table, he could walk if necessary, he can help, someone left him with me long ago, you will leave him with someone else too, at the right moment, you have to enlarge the hollow to make room for him as well, table and all."

"All right, Mr. Sima," I told him, "we'll enlarge the hollow, Zenobia and I, with our hands, we'll dig a little latrine as well, for Dragoş, people help one another, you know."

"Dragoş doesn't have any physical needs," Mr. Sima interrupted, "and he won't bother you at all, he lies still on the table, like a dead man or wax dummy, he rarely speaks, and he doesn't get up unless he has to help you with something, you know this very well, we could even do without the table, we could spread some dry twigs on the ground, or he could sleep right on the ground."

"Oh no, Mr. Sima, he's old, if he sleeps on the ground he might catch cold, please do bring the table, why shouldn't you, and so what if we have to dig with our hands, Zenobia and I, you know very well that it has to be that way, bring him, Mr. Sima, table and all, it doesn't matter."

"Well, then, I will bring him, table and all," said Mr. Sima. "When you finish enlarging the hollow I will bring him, table and all, now I have to go, it's getting dark, the wolves might come, good-bye."

Throughout our conversation, Mr. Sima cried, as is the custom on such occasions there in the blizzard, his tears froze over his eyelids, so, when he walked away, buffeted by the wind and dragging that rifle in the snow, his eyes were covered by a transparent crust, like the great blind men, like Homer, for example, and, once we'd embraced each other, we closed the window made of twigs.

10. We burrowed intensely, night and day, with our hands, Zenobia and I, until the hollow was big enough for the table, afterward we sat shoulder to shoulder by the window, we removed a few twigs and looked outside, over the snowy landscape; we knew that the first phase of our immense love was over, and we waited, like lovers await the arrival of their baby, who would bind them together differently and fill a nonexistent void, mostly to take away the caresses intended only for each other; we subjected ourselves to the curse of that strange transfer: someone was about to erode our privacy, one of our most precious commodities, and so on.

"We aren't going to love our child, are we?" I would say to Zenobia.

She chirped something about some much more powerful circles that our minds can't do anything about, she advised me, perhaps, not to place myself on their margins, lest I be thrown outside; anyway, Dragoş wasn't even a child.

And one day they came; they were walking, the two of them, through the deep snow, one behind the other, carrying that giant table, on top of which they had put the herbs and the other promised things; we let them call us, Zenobia gestured to me not to answer them, she waited until they called for the third time, then she opened the door with her own hand.

"Here I am," Mr. Sima said, "I've brought Dragoş, and the table, and the herbs, and the promised things."

This was the first time I saw Dragoş not stretched out on the table; without the dignity of the dead or the harmless soft immobility of the wax dummy, he looked like a common little old man; he wore peasant shoes made of pigskin, he wore peasant pants and a long linen shirt, his attire would have been just as natural a thousand years ago as today, in some hamlet in the mountains; he had long yellowish-gray hair down past his shoulders, he smiled in a dreadfully harmless way, bobbing his head all the time, and he jumped incessantly in the snow, maybe because of the cold.

I invited them into the hollow, and they came in, table and all, the four of us barely fit.

"It's rather smelly in here," remarked Mr. Sima, even though the door made out of twigs remained wide open.

We didn't answer him, we were looking at Dragoş and how he bobbed his head and hopped, his linen shirt rubbed against our rags, I tried to decode his dance, a kind of folk dance with extremely gentle hopping in place, like feathers floating, only a few inches above the ground, followed by brutal stomps with his right heel on the ground and accompanied by soft giggling.

"What are you doing?" I asked him, putting my hand harmlessly on his shoulder.

"I'm bouncing," he replied, bobbing his head, seemingly lost in happiness but still jumping.

"Is the old man a cretin?" I asked Mr. Sima.

"He's senile," he replied. "At his age, it couldn't be otherwise; but he helps you with vast experience, moving in the bright darkness of the mind buried in itself, like a tradition, without realizing what he is doing and why."

"Then let's put him on the table," I proposed.

"Let's do it," agreed Mr. Sima. "He won't bother you there, he'll lie still, like a dead man; but be aware that if he ever speaks, you should know that there are consonants that he won't utter, no matter what, perhaps he's forgotten them, the consonant *l* for instance; to understand what he says you might want to put the consonants back where they belong."

"I'll put them in, Mr. Sima, why shouldn't I, what would it cost me? As long as he lies still over there on his table and doesn't bother us."

I lifted Dragoş by his armpits and turned with him toward the table, he was extraordinarily light, he seemed to be filled with air, and he hopped in the air; Mr. Sima had removed the herbs and the other stuff, we installed Dragoş in their stead, and he closed his eyes and didn't move anymore.

"See how still he is?" asked Mr. Sima in admiration. "You won't even feel his presence, it will seem to you only like a vague breathing from somewhere, from your own depths, he won't bother you at all, you'll see."

"Mr. Sima," I asked, "why on earth did you bring him to me? Why didn't you take him to somebody else, why did you bequeath him to me?"

"You know very well why," replied Mr. Sima.

"No, I don't know anything, I only know that you bequeathed an old child to me, maybe I'm wrong, maybe all children are old, and it just looked otherwise, maybe he had to be born from my love and Zenobia's, I can't think of anything else."

"Then Zenobia will tell you at the right time, she probably knows; he was also brought to me by other people, that's the way it is, now I have to go, we are parting, perhaps forever, I'm going to die soon."

And Mr. Sima started to cry again, because that was the

custom on such occasions, then he came closer to Dragoș, he kissed him solemnly, I would say, on the forehead and walked out of the hollow; we didn't shut the door immediately, to freshen the air, although it was as cold as hell; Mr. Sima remained, crying, in front of the door.

"What are you doing, Mr. Sima?" I asked. "If you're not leaving, at least come back inside, I want to close the door."

"I'm waiting for my tears to freeze," he replied.

After a while, when the ice crust formed again over his eyes, he wandered away in the snow, like the great blind men; it seemed to me that he was heading in entirely the wrong direction, but I didn't have any reason to interfere and I closed the door tight behind him.

11. After that, days and weeks passed, I stayed in the dark with Zenobia, we maintained love in the world, you could hear the blizzard outside, I won't describe it, then wolves started to circle us, they whined piteously, it was, perhaps, terribly cold, a film of ice formed over the well, we had to break it when we were thirsty; sometimes we gnawed herbs, it was a state from beyond thoughts, the world's invading, desperate love had crouched there, in our rags, unfolded as far as the sun, which perhaps still existed, and beyond the sun, far away, so far away that the distance was getting lost, was forgetting to exist, was dissipating in us, in the stuffy air of the hollow; once you're here, please review those days, to fill them up with all you know about love, with all you believe you know, I'm not inventing anything, and so on.

The truth is that, for some time, Dragoș didn't bother us too much, except that he kept his eyes open, they shone like two sad stars, but one night I felt his breath on the back of my neck, a slight movement of the air made me suspect he was bobbing his head, and, by the rhythmic tremor of the twigs lying on the ground and by the rustle of his linen clothes, I realized that he was, who knows for how long, a few inches away from us; sure enough, he was there bobbing his head and jumping while listening to Zenobia's chirp; furthermore, he probably saw all that we saw in the center of the film, he probably gnawed on our herbs too, he dirtied our little latrine or, worse yet, he warmed himself in our most intimate rags.

"Listen, scum," I said (excuse me for using this word, but I don't have another one handy), "what are you doing here? Get on the table, you swine, and freeze there, if you don't want me to throw you out; why, look at him, look what he's up to! Listening to our pillow talk, spying shamelessly on our visions! Well, no, this has gone too far! Look how rude he's become, and, look, he even hops, the animal!"

"I'm code," mumbled Dragoş.

"Cold, my ass!" I yelled at him, after putting back the missing consonant, of course, "what cold, which cold? Don't you know where you are now, have you forgotten what important thing is going on here, have you forgotten why we stay crouched in this hollow? Get on the table and don't let it happen again, or else I'll break your medieval bones and throw them to the wolves to gnaw."

Truth to tell, Dragoş made it onto the table in one jump, with his eyes open, of course; but from that moment on, I started to feel cold, I gnawed on herbs all the time, my shoulder detached itself from Zenobia's shoulder; I was angry, I didn't have the least confidence in myself, in all I had seen, I felt like crying, I felt like telling Zenobia: "Can't you see how miserable I am, in this darkness and mud? Where is the world's love, where is your love? Can't you see that the smelly plastic you're wearing is cold, and you don't even love me, if you did you would do something to help me get over my fit of reason and distrust, you would rescue me from this hollow, and we too would live, like human beings, next to a warm radiator, we would ride the elevator, or we would go into a bright store, I would buy myself Irish tobacco for my pipe, not like this, in poverty, with my broken boots and my wet and frozen socks, can't you see? I'm worthless, I had this idea that I was fated, and so on, where-as you, what can I say, what the hell, maybe you are, I don't deny it, but I'm worthless, can't you see? You were wrong to choose me and you don't love me anymore, you realized that I don't deserve it, there's no point in denying it, because you don't love me anymore, that's it . . ."

Zenobia was silent, I went to the window, I moved some twigs, and I remained there for days and nights, looking outside, during the day I would see the leaden sky, the snow, and, sometimes, the wolves; then, truth to tell, I was glad that I was sheltered, I had small feelings; but during the night, when the sky was unfolding its myriad stars above us, I felt upset and small and dirty, I felt my torn shirt and my socks (likewise), I touched my forehead soiled with dirt and I felt like dying; and inside, Dragoș's eyes, shining, discouraging, and sad, were watching me.

I stayed like this for days and nights, I don't know for how long, until I felt again, against my shoulder, Zenobia's adored shoulder.

"Leave me alone," I told her, "what do you want, don't you see what I've become? I'm worthless, I'm cold, I feel like dying, I should cover my mouth with the palm of my hand and not breathe anymore, I should die and not breathe anymore, because you don't love me, I'm convinced now, and so on, I'm worthless, I have this idea about what I've seen—"

"Calm down," Zenobia said to me, now she wasn't chirping anymore, her voice was clear and melodious, "it was hard, now we've gotten past it, it's all over."

"What do you mean, 'we've gotten past it,' Zenobia, what do you mean, 'it's over'? I feel like dying, I'm desperate, and you keep saying that it's all over! Listen to her, how is it all over, when we stay buried in this mud up to our necks and I'm frozen to death, and that senile man keeps staring at me? If you don't do something to get rid of him, believe me I'll die, though you don't give a damn, I know, you were looking for men, in the swamps, believe me I'll die, right here by the window, or I'll go out to be eaten by wolves, if you don't get rid of that rotten fellow who won't take his eyes off me."

"Calm down," repeated Zenobia, and her voice sounded like a little silver bell, "calm down, leave Dragoş alone, he did what he had to do, you were between circles, on the edges, in the void, it's all over now—"

"Sure, you just say that to comfort me," I mumbled, but in fact I had calmed down already, I felt free, and I added: "I don't hold anything against Dragoş, why should I? The poor fellow lies quietly where he belongs, and I love you so unimaginably much, but it was very hard."

"Don't think about it anymore now, don't talk about it anymore," murmured Zenobia.

"I love you so unimaginably much," I told her, "and it's warm in our rags."

Then I turned from the window and I looked toward the table; naturally, Dragoş had closed his eyes.

12. Please review, while I, crouched in front of that void that I called "the window," lay in wait for the coming of spring; little by little, the snows melted, a deep serenity filled my heart when, as the snow diminished, the wet black earth appeared; puddles were left as evidence down through the valley; as far as the eye could see, a kind of undecided presentiment of grass started to cover the field with its green color, and so on; on the other side of the dam the reeds seemed to awaken and millions of dazed insects, invisible until yesterday, started their circling again, in the sunlight, which grew warmer with every passing day; from time to time I went out in front of the door to howl; I would howl two or three times, look over the field (lest somebody should hear me!), then go back inside; one day I plucked new grass, vigorous and fresh, from the dam, and I returned with my boot soles caked in cold, sticky mud.

All this time, Zenobia watched me from the hollow's

wide-open door and Dragoș continued to lie still, on the table; as a matter of fact, he hadn't opened his eyes since that day, he'd gotten terribly scared, I didn't even know whether he was still breathing; little by little, we started to go out to take care of our needs, an irrefutable sign of the approach of spring.

Gradually, my walks on the dam, through the reeds, or in the field became longer; Zenobia started to accompany me; and so, after days and nights spent in a world without dimension, what could be called "another life" began.

13. One time (it was the middle of spring by then) I was walking with Zenobia in the field, we were just mentioning this fact, when we got near the place called "The Pope's Well," I picked up a random clod from the ground.

"It's an idol," I said and, accompanied by Zenobia, I walked to a spring that I knew was nearby (not Spiridon's, which was far behind). There I dissolved the clod in the springwater and out of it came an idol made of fired clay, a rudimentary little character, who held his right hand to his mouth, as if gesturing for me to be silent (the Gumelnița culture; there is an exact replica in the Museum of the City of Bucharest). I'll add that that idol, which even now gestures to me, has the well-known holes where his ears should be and rests his right elbow in the palm of his left hand.

14. I knew a place near the forest where the swamp becomes a deep river, a while ago I rested there on the shore, with my hands I dug a chair in the dirt, the trees knew me, sometimes I asked them for the branch that I needed, a bird would come sing to me, if it stopped I asked it to continue.

To get to that place I had to go through a part of the forest, the bird showed me the way amid orange rays, if it was too damp the bird opened another way for me, but I didn't like that, I could hardly wait to get to the open field, the forest knew that and was getting upset, it wanted to scratch me, once it tried to yank out my eyes with great, ferocious love.

A field came next, the light of the horizon stopped me too abruptly, I pressed my eyelids, it was a green pasture, a few scattered oaks appeared, they gestured to each other from a distance, they had stolen out from the forest; weeds were creeping under them, they were moving, changing their places in an almost unnoticeable shifting, whole stands of them, they visited each other, maybe they made love, most of them sounded like metal wires, they told stories from a world terribly alive, my stomach contracted when listening to them because I felt unprepared for their point of view in which day and night mingled in a yellowish magma, the stars, in broad daylight, followed their course under the sun's powerful light, and at night the same thing happened, except that the light became sound.

To tear myself away from the vegetal embrace that could have annihilated me, I went out of the way along a precipice, a kind of dry riverbed about two hundred yards long, I walked with the sun on my head and with my feet in the shade, it was a riverbed of balance, there I found justifications for myself, of course they didn't count, a logic of moods pushed me toward them.

In the days before I met Zenobia, at the foot of the precipice a butterfly would greet me, usually a brown one, apparently always different but the same (I couldn't explain), sometimes it was white, it fluttered drunkenly to my left and to my right, I spoke to it in a loud voice, I thanked the butterfly as if it were an obliging guide, it kissed my eyelids, then it went away whispering to me that my coming was pleasant *to them,* a flower appeared in front of me, let's say a yellow one, I asked her how she was doing, I caressed her with my finger, a few steps away appeared the invasion of flowers she had announced, always her color, let's say yellow (other days they were mauve or blue or another color, matching the announcer's), sometimes she touched me in passing, as if to draw my attention to one of those from last time, one of the flowers, I asked her about the others, I spoke sweetly to her, she swayed rather sadly, her few remaining sisters started to show up in the most surprising places, they came out to see me, I thanked them too, I spoke to them of their sisters' dead brilliance in the city's greenhouses, and so on, until the edge of the precipice, there the field ended too, I climbed down a steep slope, some trees supported me, so I wouldn't fall down, until I reached the water.

Please review this page, mostly floral and, in any event, descriptive, while I waited for spring to set in so I could take Zenobia to that wild and tender world, indifferent to destruction, guided along the precipice by the butterfly, which was the very image, I now saw clearly, of Zenobia's smile and whispers.

15. A few days later I was wandering alone on an island, a snake was crawling near me, when I found, next to a bush, among other potsherds (the Boian culture, stupidly considered by then aniconic), a phallus of fired clay. I sat down on the trunk of a willow that had fallen in the water, I was thinking of washing the dirt off the phallus and the potsherds that I had picked up with it, the reeds concealed me on all sides, nobody could have suspected my presence there, I removed the clay fragments first, one by one, and I put them aside to dry on a thicker branch; when it was the phallus's turn, I raised, I don't know why, my eyes, and I saw coming closer, through the sparse reeds in that part, a young girl, she couldn't possibly see me, I wondered from where she had come to our deserted place, she stopped in front of me on the bank, less than twenty paces away, and lay down in the grass.

"She will stay there as long as it takes, and then she will leave," I said to myself, continuing to quietly rub that clay phallus; then I had the chance to watch, as an unseen witness, the most delirious solitary erotic exercise that I could ever have imagined; I put the phallus down, on a branch, the girl calmed down; when I picked it up again (embarrassed, because I was going through a period of extreme internal purity), it was as if I had pressed a button that triggered her madness; I repeated this a few times, so that I didn't have any doubt of the force of that object modeled thousands of years ago, until I took pity on the girl and got disgusted by my curiosity, however much it appeared to me as pure and justified; then I put the phallus aside; shortly after, the girl got up and went away without suspecting anything of this whole story.

16. Another time I was on a deserted bank, I was seized by fear, some kind of premonition-panic, I bent down to pick up something to protect myself, there were some stones around, I picked one up at random and I found myself holding in my hand a hammerhead made of shiny black granite, carved with consummate art; I started to search attentively, I wasn't frightened anymore, and, naturally, I couldn't find anything else in the area where I found the hammerhead; only, about a hundred yards away I saw, half-buried in the bank, two funeral urns (the Urn Field culture), one of them, also modeled by who-knows-what hand that had rotted millennia ago, had the hole called the "window of the soul," which even today some dwellers of the plain make in coffins so that the soul can return when it feels nostalgic for the abandoned body.

17. Please review these summary data regarding my receptiveness to a certain "mediumistic archaeology" for which I had the displeasure of being mentioned in a work on inscriptions on Greek amphora handles as the discoverer of a hypothetical Apollonia, a hard-to-find fortress; I say what can be said at the moments when the little idol takes his finger away from his lips, and I'm interested neither in funeral

urns nor in black hammers nor in clay phalli; but as the things accounted for so far could suggest a solicitation force applying specifically only to ancient objects, I might feel tempted to mention my connections with other objects, for example, a pipe lost twice in the seventeen-hundred-acre stretch of the swamp, which, after a few days, inexplicably returned to me, should I say, walking by herself (every now and then I talk to her, I kiss her, she's fond of me); I could enumerate, exactly as they happened, so many things, but I won't do it, out of decency; besides, related to my aforementioned receptiveness, and seeing no difference at all between states and facts, I'm writing here (because it seems that I am writing) about love, and I like the mumbling that dissolves my intelligence and my culture in order to open other doors for me, I like the blade of grass, the cat, and the little stick that know exactly the state of affairs, I like the idea that you will ignore, one more time, all these things and take them for granted.

18. After a while, the waters brought me a rotten boat, one of those coffins that are built by the peasants in those parts—made out of a few boards held together by a few nails and smeared with pitch—and using a pole as an oar, I started to scour the swamp. Many times, stretched out in the boat, I listened to the noise of water, wind, reeds, or living things, I won't enumerate them, I will only say that, all together, they made up the buzzing silence of that deserted place; but once I heard a kind of a strange grunt, whose origin, in spite of my receptiveness, was impossible for me to determine; then, after another grunt, a little more substantial, a voice, unmistakably human, shouted from somewhere on the other side of the reeds: "Hey, who's stinking up the swamp?"

There were indisputably humans there, but, with the exception of that lonely young girl, I never saw them face to face.

If it happened to rain during the long wanderings, where I was empty of thoughts but full of a fertile integration into the core of the film, lost among the tracks through the reeds now the color of turquoise, I pulled the boat onto the bank and, turning it over, took shelter in the inner vapor, while the sky thundered above. On my way back, I headed always in the direction of the immense red sun, toward the end of the dam, where Zenobia's crystal silhouette awaited me.

"I was worried," she said to me, "I was afraid that something might have happened to you; when it's the two of us, I don't care, we can die together."

I confess that her fear seemed incomprehensible to me and I didn't realize how she could have had, even for an instant, the feeling of separation; but by having to a certain extent the intuition of what was swarming beyond the appearances of the common human malady, I held the conviction that she, the great free lover, couldn't have been mistaken.

In fact, I doubted somewhat my truths, gross enough, behind which I knew there were others, ready at any time to dismiss my truths, and still other truths that were capable of destroying the latter, including the first ones, which were flimsy enough too, but all, absolutely all, were trustworthy.

19. Naturally, I'm not talking (or writing—because it seems that I am writing) about truths as such here but about truths of any kind, even those that I overlook, although they seem extremely important to me; they guarantee their own active existence especially by their refusal to let themselves be expressed, a refusal that belongs to us and not to them, because it is indifferent to them, and so on. What I'm saying sounds a little complicated; anyway, I won't insist on it, I'll only say that after one of my not-at-all-meditative wanderings, I recited to Zenobia:

"As you know, my dear, I'm what you could call an urbanite; I was born and raised on the streets of Bucharest, there I completed my, pardon me, studies and completed a year or two of military service in the stables of a cavalry regiment; there I had the premonition of our encounter, even the certainty, I might say, and I wrote a book that nobody understood much of, outside of some intelligent references to Nerval or others, which was in no way like me; back then I lived on 5 Leonida Street but later I moved into the vestibule of a young lawyer on Well-with-Poplars Street, on the corner of Astronomer Street, he had a dog made of stone at the foot of the stairs and an Italian landlord; please review: in the evening first a brunette and then a blonde knocked on my window, you would have sworn that I was visited by a Spaniard and a Swede, respectively, both of them brought me apples, but let's drop it . . . Then I moved to a corridor, on the ninth or tenth floor, and so on. But now, I don't know why, I would like to go for a walk around the city, to see how the people are bustling about there; it is, anyway, one reason, and I would like you to come with me."

"Very well," said Zenobia, "let's go but let's take Dragoş with us, we can't leave him alone."

It so happened that that day we unbundled the package of things given to us by Mr. Sima. Zenobia found the dress and a little rabbit fur; the dress, rotten and yellowed by time, came down over her heels, Zenobia put it on after nicely folding and putting on the table the sheet of plastic, now brownish but still sturdy; she refused the little fur because it was terribly hot at the time, and, as there were no shoes in the package, she kept the footwear that I wove out of rushes to protect her soles.

I pulled on the blue trousers Mr. Sima had given me, and the ruffled shirt and the white boots, and, in order to be elegant in the world of the city, toward which we were heading, I fastened the little rabbit fur around my neck; after that, I shook Dragoş.

He woke up immediately and started to hop and to bob his head.

"Quit hopping," I told him, "we're going to town."

He stopped hopping and sat down obediently on the grass, on the crest of the dam; then, naturally, he zealously helped us cover, as best we could, the entrance of the hollow with boulders; for that I rewarded him with the fur cap; after that, we set off toward the city, the three of us, Zenobia and I shoulder to shoulder and Dragoş behind us.

That day, in the swamps, the last cranes were returning.

II

■ □ ■ □ ■

THE CITY

1. WHEN WE ARRIVED AT THE GATES OF THE CITY IT WAS
raining just like now—pouring, that is—Zenobia's long dress
dragged heavily through the mud, her rush sandals splashed
it in all directions, even though she stepped so lightly that
she barely touched the ground; as for Dragoş, water streamed
from his wet fur cap over his long wet hair, over his wet shirt
down to his soaked peasant shoes; from time to time I, for
one, would wring out the fringes of my ruffles, I would have
liked to smoke, it wasn't possible in that situation, and I was
feeling good, warmed by Zenobia's closeness and our care
for the senile old man who walked behind us as if dancing.

Once downtown, we sat on the curb, in the rain. Cars
and people raced in all directions, and I said to Zenobia:
"Listen, my dear, I'm afraid we might catch cold and I
believe we're hungry, we should eat something and find shelter, don't you think?"

"We'd need money for that," said Zenobia, with remark-
able practicality. "Let's look, who knows, perhaps we can
find some."

We wandered through the streets, that would have been a
solution, we found only two or three coins, in times past we
had found more but not now, so we finally gave up.

"Zenobia," I said, "hunger doesn't bother me, it puts me
in that pleasurable state, but you are frail and Dragoş has to
be sheltered, I can see that you just don't care, because if you

did you would find a solution, tomorrow I'll take care of everything, I have enough connections in this city; even though the majority of the population is ignorant of me, there are people who appreciate me, boys and girls our age, tomorrow I'll find shelter for Dragoş, and I'll obtain some apples for you, but right now I'm convinced that you just don't care about us."

Here it seems necessary to mention my then erroneous opinion that Zenobia let appearances unfold a little bit too freely, as well as my equally erroneous need to try to stimulate her, a need due more to my naïveté and lack of confidence in myself, not in her. At such moments I talked as I just did (I was only talking but sometimes I got mad, really mad) and she, as though she had committed an indecency, performed, when I least expected it, one of those small miracles that generally seem to us amazingly banal and unimportant, related to a false immediate causality and maintained within the limits of the admissible, in a zone of ambiguity capable at any time of accepting the most natural and modest explanations.

This time she put her hand into a little pocket of her dress (she hadn't even noticed it until then) and found some small change, apparently left by Mr. Sima, it wasn't much, but we didn't even wish for much money, and then we went to the market, we went into a tavern, we ate something, standing at the counter, Dragoş was watching us, smiling, I wasn't mad anymore, I even felt like laughing.

By the time we left the tavern the rain had stopped, the streetlights were throwing their misty lights over the asphalt, and then Maria passed by, Maria whom I had visited now and then, before my departure for the swamps.

"Gellu!" she exclaimed. "Where have you been all this time?"

"I've been in the country," I said. "I've been doing fine there."

"You've lost weight," she said, then she looked at Zenobia, she eyed her from head to toe, she saw there was steam coming out of her or smoke, she didn't seem to see Dragoş.

"And where are you going now?"

"I have no idea," I answered. And I added: "Good-bye, Maria."

"Come stay at my place," she proposed. "I have a new studio, it's not far, it's vacant."

"Sorry, Maria," I said, "but now I am, so to speak, engaged, and she's my fiancée and this fellow wearing the fur hat is my friend, so good-bye."

"You both can come," said Maria (she continued to ignore Dragoş), "at least for a cup of coffee."

"Your invitation is tempting, Maria," I said, "but you know that I can't stand what you paint, those haystacks, and so on; two years ago when I used to visit you at your studio on Xenopol Street, you were prepared, you would first turn the paintings to the wall so I couldn't see them and get mad."

"I can still turn them," she answered, sighing. "All you have to do is wait a few minutes at the door until I turn them."

We went with her to 12 Willows Street, in the backyard where she had her new studio, a pleasant enough room, she didn't live there, she came there only to work, she painted stupid landscapes, we waited outside until she turned the canvases, then we walked in, she fixed coffee for Zenobia and me, she still seemed to ignore Dragoş. Maria told us that we could use the studio for a while, until we found a place, I politely invited her to leave us alone because we were tired, and she left.

"Tomorrow," I said to Zenobia, after we turned off the lights and stretched out on the sofa while Dragoş settled in on Maria's long table over old paint tubes and piled-up canvases, "tomorrow I'll obtain some apples for you too."

---

*The perfectly preserved bodies of seven pilots who disappeared over Iceland 28 years ago were discovered in a glacier.

2. We stayed at Maria's place for a while, I don't know how long, she had cared for me in her own way since the time when I used to play rugby, she used to come to the field just to see me, she maintained that she liked my pohems a lot too, after we moved in she came to see us again for several days, she had fallen on the street, she had hurt her head, she had broken a tooth, she would come without it, she would cover her mouth with her hand, she would bring me books to read, she would lean against the table where Dragoş was sleeping, she wouldn't say a word; Zenobia would push her aside, softly and gently, with her hand, like a curtain, every time she was in the way, Maria would say nothing, she would sigh, she would stroke her mouth with her index finger, then she would briskly go out, almost running, it seemed to me that she was crying.

3. Please review all this without paying too much attention to a particular aggressiveness that might show in my gestures and my speech; in the swamps I had even been hit in the stomach without retaliating, then I moaned because I had to, while waiting for someone to crouch for all of us; but there I was dominated by the open evidence of the great rhythms that we lose, whereas in the magma of the city, despair and anger, otherwise vain, are harder to melt; however, I would like to state that here again my deceptive abruptness and my apparent cynicism are no more than the unimportant stridency of a underground serenity tougher than all the angers of the world; and I add that it shouldn't appear strange, for example, to state that in those days that I write about (because it seems that I am writing) I could have brazenly opened my fly in front of Maria, considering her as something that sighs and nothing more.

Besides, to protect my purity from the squalid idea of a virginal state, I'll add that, having loved intensely since I was four and a half, as I'm assured by the unsure data of my memory, I've had enough lovers in the course of time, although I didn't look for them on purpose, oh, how they loved me, how they hated me!

There was one, for example, now she's a distinguished doctor of medicine, back then she was a student, she was completing her training in a hospital in a small provincial town, I was living temporarily in the woods, I would come to see her on horseback, I would see her in the park, I would tie the horse to an ancient tree, I would walk her to the inferno, she would be happy; when I saw her again, after some time, on a streetcar, in a big city, she said that she had two children and that she hated me with all her heart, she was the same, she couldn't forget the inferno, she said: "You ruined my life, my husband is a nice, capable man, but at night, when I pull the blanket over my head to be alone, I'm haunted by the memory of those days, etc." She wanted to kill me, mind you, to throw me off the moving streetcar.

There was another one, she worked for a foreign film distributor, she would take me for rides in a brougham, in winter, she would send me white lilacs, we would embrace on a swing, I would walk her to paradise, she was happy; when we met again, many years later, she hated me with all her soul, she looked knives and daggers at me, she said exactly what the other one had said, I won't repeat it, that's the way it happens every time, one way or another, each one thought that she had loved, I myself had thought the same until Zenobia appeared, I could have died, I could have committed suicide, mind you, convinced that I was doing it for love, not knowing that to a few, to a very few only, is it given to know the miracle, don't worry, I'm not talking of something else, while Maria was bringing me books to read and was silent in her conviction that she too might love me, it seemed to me that she was crying, that was her business . . .

*The Kitt Peak Observatory announced the discovery of the remains of a star that exploded approximately 300,000 years ago in the Cygnus constellation.

THE CITY

4. Like a corpse with the wings of an angel was Maria, she dropped by to see us less and less often, her eyes protruded slightly, I liked her, she moved giddily in this world, she managed pretty well, her parents helped her too; once, when she met me alone in the street (I had gone out to get some apples), she stopped me and held my hand for about an hour, she kept covering her mouth with her hand, she kept looking down, she wouldn't say a word.

"Maria," I tried to explain to her, because ultimately she was a sensible girl, "you should know that some time ago it occurred to me to play backgammon with someone even though I don't like this game and I don't care whether I win or lose; I was only interested in the dice I threw; and imagine that sometimes I managed to enter into contact with the dice, I was in some kind of a state, I won't insist, actually I would then say in my mind 'four-two' or 'five-three' or whatever, and I would throw exactly what I had thought; sometimes I would say out loud 'Let me throw a four-three or a five-two,' or whatever, and I would throw them exactly, to the amazement of my opponent, who would say 'Well, look at that, you throw them as if on command'—that would happen to me in my moments of weakness or petty vanity only, and then the other man had me throw the dice from a cup, which didn't matter at all; but there were other days when everything would end up the other way around, when I would throw with my own hand exactly the dice that shouldn't have been thrown, understand? I knew the numbers in advance, I would name them in my mind, fearful and hopeful that I wouldn't throw them and I was thinking of where I went wrong, outside the game, of course; I was worried by my tendency and my capacity for harming myself, the fact that I was again becoming a two-willed being, even though I considered that I had gotten rid of that, anyway, I won't go into details; however, I felt saddened, the other man was convinced that I was saddened by the outcome of a wretched game, he had his point of view also, how could I possibly explain this to him? Look, I'm standing here like a cretin and I'm babbling all these profoundly true stupidities, which I'm sure you don't believe, or, if you do, they don't matter too much to you because you have your point of view, why wouldn't you, like any human being? The bad part is that this point of view of yours makes you cry, and I'll shut up, it's your business . . ."

Like a corpse with the wings of an angel was Maria, holding my hand there in the street, where I had met her, when in fact I had gone out to get some apples . . .

5. Before leaving for the swamps I happened to read the newspapers now and then, but I couldn't stand their vulgarity and monstrous pornography. (Maybe it should be added that the pornography mentioned here has nothing in common with sexuality, to which it was linked for centuries, only to spoil one of the last opportunities left to humans to recover the lost breezes of the beginning; it should be added that the aforementioned pornography ferments in the aberrations of the public's common sense and especially in the unprecedented aggressiveness of the powers, but let's drop it . . .)

Sometimes, however, to get even more disgusted, I would read the newspapers; this sporadic occupation didn't really deprive me of the hours devoted to reading the tomes of the era, real urinals solidly built and equipped with subtle and ultraperfected fixtures, out of whose faucets theory flowed, poetry whispered, it made you want to vomit, really; they were stiff, ready to seize you between their wooden jaws; I used to read them stubbornly, from cover to cover, I wouldn't skip a line: "Since I've begun, I have to go all the way," I would say to myself, this was one of the severest tests that I imposed on myself, and so on.

The sporadic reading of newspapers offered a compensation too: their misery allowed a certain superficiality, a relaxing one most of the time: I would read just the headlines and the first words of the articles and, if I intuited in them something of interest, I would cut out the articles with scissors and paste them on a white sheet of paper; this way, every few months or so, when I had gathered more fragments that had escaped from the unconscious-intentional pornography of the whole, I could read an ad hoc bulletin, where the news, used mostly as filler, became rather instructive because I found in it things and facts upon which one could meditate.

I should also add that at each reading of the bulletin I was surprised at, among other things, the persistent poverty of the collective fantasy, if I may express myself this way; beside some extremely rare and old obsessions, the ultrascarce amount of news demonstrated, even back then, that this field was either in a period of impasse, which wouldn't be cause for surprise, or had moved its proofs of manifestation to other, still obscure, zones.

Anyway, to me the phenomenon appeared closely linked to the mutations of the aforementioned pornography, amen.

I mention all this to explain the interpolation in this text of some excerpts from my news report, reproduced as they appeared in newspapers; they are marked by an asterisk and, however fragile their causal relationship might appear, they belong to the larger circles of my movements back then . . .

*The young painter Bruno Mendoza, 23, ended his creative period at the bottom of a grotto that he left after three days and two nights, returning with the nine canvases and 27 drawings he had made in the semidarkness.

6. Maria's studio resembled, to some extent, Mr. Sima's upstairs room. Zenobia even asserted that it was the same room, even the window, although it didn't overlook the swamps, was in its place.

Here, on a little red shelf placed to the left of the window, a few objects were assembled; the need to enumerate them that I experience right now is not essentially descriptive in nature. It belongs, perhaps, to a preparatory ritual meant to reunite what, in an apparent way, divides. Here are the objects:

A glass bowl: empty, round, and transparent. To its left, an archaic statuette: Cybele seated; time had eroded her features, multiplying them under the veils of effacement that emphasize her melancholy indifference; serene and calm, she rests her hands in her lap.

To her left, a lion looking tensely to his left; the top of his head, with mane and all, doesn't extend above Cybele's waist.

Above them, made of grayish metal and hanging on the wall, a Gothic letter *U*.

Under the shelf, an old key, a little bigger than regular keys . . .

*Wishing to transform his yard into a silent and harmless zoo, John Fairnington of Branxton populated it with animals made of concrete.

7. On the first day of my stay at Maria's place, I found in front of the door, on the outer threshold, a moth. Its heavy and fluffy body as big as a sparrow's chick throbbed intermittently, and then it remained stock-still, its wings unfolded. To save it from the night's cold blades I took it, not without disgust, and put it in a box on the table below the window.

(I should add a few details about the red cardboard box that, according to my habit of naming things, I called "Intimacy," but I fear rendering more difficult an understanding that is vague enough already.)

The next morning, a hostile Rhythm circled me: it vibrated, chirped, buzzed, struck the windowpane, crackled in the whitewash of the walls, I felt it everywhere, real and perfidious.

To protect myself, I started to swing my head right and left, it was a threat, the Rhythm diminished, compressed, and became a rustle, more and more localized, a fingernail that lightly scratched the interior of the cardboard box on the table.

Then I remembered the butterfly, I took Intimacy and opened it; the butterfly came out, it was still alive, it tried to crawl heavily toward a darker corner, I threw it out.

The next day I found aligned on the threshold *six* butterfly wings, all the same, I recognized them immediately, they were its wings, all six of them, there was no trace left of the rest of the body. I burned them where I had found them.

The third morning, when I wanted to go out, I found them, the six wings, again, carefully set in order on the outer threshold, undoubtedly the same, I burned them again, then I returned to the studio, I sat on a chair facing the wall and I started to wait, I knew I had to wait . . .

8. Naturally, I say only what is appropriate, apparently petty things, that is—aware of the fact that even they sometimes seem a little far-fetched, this being their way of allowing themselves to be seen; it is as if I were trying to narrate a mountain with its avalanches and all, but only a pebble would let itself be narrated—or the fog at the edge of the precipice; but I'm convinced that even in their silence the moan of the struggle between peak and abyss can sometimes be distinguished.

Also, by accounting for these hard-to-accept things I'm not trying to untangle the texture in which I squirmed more or less blinded by my own retinas: in the beginning I persisted in understanding, in the ordinary sense of the word, but that understanding could only touch echoes that arrived from very far away, hardly flickering like vanishing rays; in the course of time, explanations turned into openings for new traps, born out of themselves.

*Marc de Maere, who stayed for 105 days in a specially outfitted coffin one and one-half yards underground, is preparing to spend 206 days in similar conditions.

9. In those days I also managed to obtain, besides apples, a minute quantity of cornmeal; the latter, boiled with a lot of water, became gruel; left to cool, it constituted our basic food, a horrible one, I should say, which would have deeply disgusted us if we had taken notice of it.

Anyway, the permanent euphoric state in which we lived back then could have been blamed on our nutrition, an explanation that was, as I realized later, the most logical, the most cretinous.

No doubt about it, our receptiveness, particularly Zenobia's, could have easily solved the little miseries of life, but we didn't even think of using it for such needs; and if we did, once or twice, put a coin in a public telephone or public scales and come away with a heap of small change, this was a game for us: we realized that it was possible and, without being surprised or repeating it, we let it be possible.

10. Everything was happening according to the laws of a strange active indifference; thanks to it, the most insignificant gestures gained in importance while the limits of the conscious will grew more and more unstable: anything that happened seemed at the same time constant and reversible, certain and treacherous, but we'd better change the subject . . .

In those days Zenobia adapted to the new conditions of our existence; it was a fluid adaptation in ordinary life that didn't differ at all from prefigured life; she would pour one into the other, her gestures and words aligned themselves in an obscure and even modesty that only the remains of my vanity tried, on occasion, to oppose.

For me, Zenobia represented the untrammeled marvelous; her naïveté and fears were of a different nature: she could be startled and frightened by a rustle, she heard the movement of shadows on the walls.

*In Venezuela, members of an expedition accidentally discovered a forest growing in an underground cave. The forest, composed of broad-leaved trees so tall and dense that special axes had to be used to cut a path through it, has green foliage in which chlorophyll forms even though the rays of the sun do not penetrate the underground cave.

11. Zenobia outran my gestures and intentions; I don't know whether her point of view coincided with mine, although it might be said that we weren't living individually; but *our* point of view, always coinciding, was something other than a coincidence.

I had the impression that even her silences spoke to me about something that I had known for a long time, something impossible to formulate in words, usually experienced like a reconciliation, like a total and calm knowledge.

She protected me from explanations; we both knew that it wasn't necessary to formulate but to live according to that prefigured world and to become in this way receptive to it; when we succeeded, the chaotic conflict of some elements and ideas dissolved, the apparent disorder gained coherence; but this required sufficient pain and suffering: in order to bear them, my surface of contact, still fragile back then, often obliged me to resort to poetry; then the incoherent and the ambiguous entered the game only as appearances of the possible, while, on the contrary, the formulated under-standing appeared to me to be half lost.

Zenobia helped me to reestablish, step by step, a partially forgotten, partially prefigured nature, but one that entitled me to doubt the reality of my perceptions; this nature con-stituted for her the natural field of existence.

In the cloud that lived us the time of theory had passed, it was a time of proofs and testimonies; there, the solicita-tions, especially those regarding the state and movement of the world, disconnected themselves in order to be reconnected differently and their new connections made room for others, infinitely enriched, they became something else, remaining, in a way, the same.

I knew that the obsession of a hidden significance of things, like any other obsession, was largely due to unreceptiveness and that the obsessive state, as the explanation of the significance, could only lead to a new myopia, to a new ᵨystematized error. Zenobia knew the anger and frustration that systems caused me.

*For 33 years now, Dr. William Bean has carefully kept track of the growth rhythm of his left thumbnail.

12. Zenobia read my thoughts, all my thoughts; once, we both stood silent, Dragoş was sleeping on the table; I was reading something on that listener and confidante of the innermost depths, Sister Mechtilde of Magdeburg, who, about a millennium ago, haunted by visions of the inferno, announced the coming reign of everlasting hate.

"Why everlasting *hate*?" Zenobia asked me.

"How do you know?" I said.

"Know what?"

"About Mechtilde—"

"What Mechtilde?" Zenobia asked; and when I told her what I was reading, she confessed that she knew nothing about any Mechtilde but she couldn't stand hate; she spoke up just like that, at random, and she seemed to be more amazed than I, even more frightened, you might have said that she wanted to apologize.

*The Pacific beaches of Peru were invaded by giant jellyfish of all colors, yanked from the depths by storms.

13. On another occasion, when we got two tickets for the circus, I unwittingly ruined the show of a poor hypnotist.

He performed with a young man of our age who had to guess, blindfolded, the ID numbers of the people in the audience, and so on. That night Zenobia and I were in a good mood, we always liked circus performances, so I jokingly asked Zenobia, "What if I make the boy come to me?"

Zenobia burst out laughing, I immediately forgot what I'd said, it didn't matter to me, when that blindfolded young man bumped into me, right at the end of the hall where I was seated; this was repeated three or four times, I didn't know how to get rid of him, much to the hypnotist's despair, until the audience started to boo; another act followed, and then another, till the end . . .

"Your performance was very good," said Zenobia on our way home, seemingly trying to remove the unpleasant aftertaste caused by my pitiful exhibition.

*Twenty-eight-year-old Michel Lottito succeeded in eating almost an entire 15-pound bicycle in 12 days.

14. I stood in my cloud and looked; actually, I didn't look for anything, I stood as if in transparent vapor, days passed slowly, I hardly went out at all. Zenobia was always missing, she maintained that she had to work as well. In the endless night of the world the same wolves howled, the same stars shone.

On one of those days, in the late afternoon, Zenobia advised me to get some fresh air, to go for a walk. "You're so pale," she said, "go buy some yellow blotting paper or whatever you want."

I went out, it was clouding over, there was a little stationery store nearby, Zenobia had mentioned the names of some streets, I had to go only that way, if I made a detour, something else would move.

I walked through the all-too-familiar streets, I saw as through a mist people with white or green faces, there were some houses, someone shouted from an open window:

"Ioana-a-a!" a woman dropped some coins as I passed by, I heard them clinking, she bent down to pick them up from the pavement, I was going to buy yellow blotting paper or whatever I wanted.

Then, without reason, I turned away; drops of rain began to fall, a cloud shed water, to my left was Palade Street, a quiet little street, above it the sky seemed to be a giant tent hung with blue planets that floated calmly from horizon to horizon, it couldn't possibly rain there; I had the feeling that I had gone down a cemetery path, a trace of weakness made me vaguely wonder why I had deviated from my route, what I was doing on a cemetery path.

Years ago, I used to walk to school on that street. On my way I would stick my tongue out at people, if there was a lame person there, I would walk ahead of him and limp; but now, after a few steps, I saw coming toward me, from the other end of the street, one of my friends, he gestured to me from afar, he seemed to be coming to a meeting that had been scheduled in advance.

That friend, whose name I never knew and, I think, never will, was a rather tall boy, rather blond, I have the impression that he always wore white shirts with an open collar, anyone would have said that he was good looking. I met him for the first time at the Northern Railroad Station, some time before my leaving for the swamps, I was in the second-class waiting room, I was sitting on a bench, I haven't the slightest idea why I was there, anyway, I didn't want to go anywhere, I simply waited, it was crowded, hundreds of people . . .

I saw him, over the crowd, at the other end of the room, apparently he was looking for someone too; when he noticed me he raised his arm, he was still on the threshold, he waved to me; I raised my arm too, I was waiting for him; he came toward me, we embraced, he sat beside me on the bench, we talked for several hours, he said that he made some kind of measurements for a living (of fields or roads, I didn't understand), I told him a few things about myself too, we were both convinced that we knew each other from the beginning of time, he addressed me by name (he had given me a nonsensical name, I believe he called me "Scarlat," I didn't contradict him, it didn't matter at all), only when he left did I realize that I had met him for the first time and that I had forgotten to ask him his name.

Now, on Palade Street, my nameless friend stretched out his hand to me and quickly said: "I've been waiting for you at the cemetery."

"At the cemetery? What would I be doing at the cemetery?" I asked, surprised.

He looked at me for a second, and then he said: "Going to the funeral; Constantin died."

Then he hastily shook my hand and left; it started to rain on Palade Street, I hadn't had the time to ask him how he knew Constantin, how he knew that I knew him too, it didn't matter, I went to buy yellow blotting paper or whatever I wanted.

When I got back home, I told Zenobia about my deviating from the route and all; actually, I would tell her every evening about everything I did during the day, reviewing in this way my usual swings between the miseries of vanity and the pettiness of modesty; usually she wouldn't say anything, I had to reach the end alone, she was silent then too, but because she was beside me everything seemed clear in our circles.

*In Grenoble, Christian Schaller was attacked with karate chops by two women, who, after taking his documents and his wallet, which contained 800 francs, disappeared, by all accounts, in a car with two men inside.

15. It is extremely hard for me to locate Zenobia in her real surroundings, not because I don't want to but because most of the time words obscure what they mean to say; poor makeup over the paleness of a face could not bring into view

anything of her inner tenderness; moreover, she nags almost all day long (she's been nagging ever since she played with her rag dolls as a little child), she talks to herself, and she is amazingly slow; moreover, she is extremely harsh and gentle, at the same time.

16. For Zenobia there is nothing unimportant or common; in this respect she is like a magnifying glass in which the world changes size, naturally and by itself, in slow patterns, and doesn't strive to exist; through her, eclipses disappear in an all-absorbing clarity, for, later, a simple word of hers regarding some banal household concern suffices to recall them there again, where you wouldn't even suspect that they would be possible.

In all this, she remains a well-behaved and naive little girl; but sometimes she is extremely obstinate, she keeps saying no and only no; then all my arguments become useless and some time has to pass for me to understand that the opposition was due to "my transient departure from the circles," to use her own words. Naturally, moments like these would deeply affect me if they didn't also contain the comforting thought that, from all those people, she has chosen me.

Actually, Zenobia maintains that everything I do is very important and she grieves every time I lose my self-confidence; she is convinced that my life path requires me to advance, whatever it takes, on it alone, and that along the path there is, at any moment, the thing toward which I'm moving, even though, sometimes, I happen to forget or ignore it.

17. I was humiliated by this poor, profanatory description of Zenobia. Because of this I haven't written a line for several days; I should have known, however, from the very start, that I'm defiling a zone that, due to my structure and habits, allows itself to be described, and vaguely enough at that, only through what I call a "pohem." I shouldn't have forgot-

ten that otherwise the temptation of describing her even a little entails texts, the hand-crafted innocence of which has only one merit: that of placing me outside literature . . .

18. Before leaving for the swamps I used to go on long walks without a precise goal. Some hard-to-define impulse announced to me the moment I had to set out. Then I would board the first train, the direction didn't matter, or the first bus, and when I had gotten eight or ten miles from the city, I would return home on foot.

In the summertime, when I grew tired or when the heat of the sun became unbearable, I slept in railroad stations, under acacia trees, on the grass. Usually my trips ended near some place full of relics or at the bottom of an abandoned sand quarry, I liked to look at the exposed faults, I would read them like the pages of a book, there were old bones too.

In the wintertime, the wind whipped my cheeks on the empty highways, the almost frozen sparrows accompanied me with screams of fear, I would put some of them under my overcoat, they would stay there until they had warmed themselves, then they would fly off and scream again, leaving room for others.

It so happens that while we were living at Maria's place, I felt that impulse and I told Zenobia that I had to go, I didn't know where; it was near midnight, she put some food, a fistful of tobacco, a matchbox, and a little paint-stained spatula in one of Maria's bags.

At the railroad station, the first train was leaving for the Bărăgan plains. I bought a round-trip ticket for the distance that I could afford with the little money that I had in my pocket, I don't remember to what station, and I boarded a third-class coach.

As we traveled, the few passengers talked among themselves in whispers, as if not to disturb the night. I crouched on a bench, waiting to know where I had to get off. An hour later I knew and I got off.

It was a way station, I couldn't read its name, a wooden booth with an almost extinguished lamp, blackened with smoke. The train had stopped for a few moments, I barely had time to get off.

I knocked on the window of the booth, someone inside whispered: "What do you want?" I asked, also whispering, where the village was, I didn't mention its name because I didn't know it, the voice from the booth answered: "Go straight ahead, the road will take you there," a road loomed in the pitch-darkness, next to the booth, I walked along it for a while, under scattered trees, then I turned away, over the fields, it had started to drizzle, I heard on another road, maybe nearby, maybe faraway, people whispering to their cattle and carts squeaking; it was a wet darkness, I came across a trail, I knew that I had to go that way, and it took me to village lanes that seemed endless to me; I struck out blindly to the left and to the right with the bag in my hand to protect myself, never before had so many silent and furious dogs rushed upon me, they thrust their fangs in my bag, one remained stuck with his teeth in it, I whirled the bag around in the air, cur and all, to throw it off, I was certain that people were watching me from their dark houses, it seemed to me that I heard their whispers, but no one came out to drive the pack away.

At the edge of the village I stopped to catch my breath, the dogs stayed behind, I could hear their muffled growls; then I took a shortcut across a plowed field and stopped next to a cluster of acacia trees. I knew that that was the place: a hole, a kind of deep and not very long ditch. I jumped in the hole, I crouched on its bottom, I was soaked in perspiration, the drizzle had wet my clothes, my eyes closed with sleepiness and fatigue.

After a while the sky cleared; I would be startled from time to time and look up, the stars sparkled and they seemed to jump to and fro, the whole celestial vault spun silently above me; I groped on the bottom of the hole until I found something, then I fell asleep.

THE CITY

When I woke up it was already dawn. I set off to go back to the way station. The dogs had calmed down. I went through the village without seeing a living soul, you would have thought that they had all died. My wet clothes, now scorched by the sun, had started to burn me. Back at the way station, I knocked on the window again. The lamp had turned off by itself, I think. I asked at what time the first train for Bucharest came by, the same voice whispered to me that I had to wait some more. The sun had become a reddish-yellow explosion. I went over to the side, there was a stand of acacia trees there too, I lay down in their shade.

At home I offered Zenobia the shiny stone medallion polished some three thousand years ago and recovered by me for her from the darkness of the hole; she says that that black stone has always been hers and she still wears it occasionally on a small, thin strap around her neck.

*In Montemesola the annual competition for the most beautiful mustache was won by the Greek, Nicolas Stassinos, the owner of a 24-inch mustache.

19. At first, when you put your finger on a thing and that thing lights up, it's not at all funny, you're even scared; usually, after that, the requital starts, with the hardly discernible subtleties of consciousness, the torture of uncertainty starts, whether you only foresaw the lighting up or whether it just occurred when your finger touched it.

It is difficult to get used to the thought that you could have a longer or a shorter leg than the others, you are limping, in any case, and the cheap compensation of singularity is no comfort.

At such moments, Zenobia would come into my cloud, she would whisper something, she would learn nothing from me and would teach me nothing, we were each lived by our common universe, we naturally understood one another, without too many words.

After that she would smile, she would forget, I would forget too, outside it was getting dark, that's how we stood, embracing, in the middle of the room, no noise, no ray of light came in from outside, I lay on the sofa.

"Zenobia," I said, "I wrote some stupid pohems, would you read them to me? They're over there, on the table . . ."

She picked up the papers, she lay beside me in the dark, I think that she closed her eyes too, the darkness became warm and soft. Zenobia read with her fingertips, words dripped first clear and then muddy, I intuited exactly which ones had gotten to the other side.

At other times, when my pohems bored me (I felt that every brake-letter, every word meant to turn me around, to return the angel to the communal toilet of the mental realm, and I wandered in the immense desert of requital), I asked her to read to me from any old book left behind by Maria. One time, she came across some poems in Flemish. Then, her slightly frightened voice whispered to me in the dark: "They're in a foreign language . . ."

"It doesn't matter," I said. "It's even better . . ."

She passed her fingers over the pages and she started to read, the sounds seemed strange to our ears, but we understood their meaning, from beyond words.

20. One of those days, while Zenobia was out, Maria visited us, she hadn't dropped by in a long time, she brought some roses in bloom, she said they were from her garden.

"I won't stay long," she said, "I don't want to bother you . . ."

"You can stay as long as you want," I told her. "You're not bothering me, you're in your own home. You know, I hope we'll move out soon—"

"There's no hurry," she said, moving softly, and she emanated so much warmth and submission that any boy would have at least kissed her. "I came to get some old drawings, I didn't know you were alone."

"But I'm not alone, Maria," I said pointing vaguely toward the table where Dragoş, who hadn't opened his eyes in a long time, was watching us with an alert curiosity, "there's the old man too" (now Dragoş frowned a little and shook his head, as if scolding me).

Maria looked toward the table and then she turned to me, confused.

There are people with whom it is pleasant to chat, they incite you, they give you the impression that they understand very well what you say and what you don't say, often they disappoint you as well, it happened to me too; anyway, they don't bore you, you don't have to explain all the time, it seems that they understand you at once, you don't even have time to finish your sentence.

To me, Maria belonged to those people, that's why, not to remain silent, I told her immediately that I liked music, especially the music of crickets, I told her about those two well-diggers who talked to each other, from the well each was digging, and depending on the layer that he reached, one well-digger sat on clay, the other on sand, that's their business; I also told her about a nonexistent sculptor by the name of Heraclitoris, whose grandmother lived in a valley burned by the sun, and about a collective suicide plan where we all would die on a beach, hitting ourselves in the head with a shoe. "There is, however, a compensation," I said, "but it is to be found in locker rooms, where we give new names to the same ancient and lamentable errors," and so on.

That's how I talked with Maria and I was feeling good, that emptiness with vague demarcations filled itself with lukewarm effluvia, I was listening to myself as if to a stranger, not always satisfied with myself, I found justifications for myself: "I don't want to give her time to unfold herself, she would bore me too much, I prefer to hear my own mind foundering," my acceptable pose was relaxing.

Maria was listening to me, she seemed to perfectly understand the unfortunate drop of phosphorus that was still sparkling among the sounds, she stood next to the table by the window, she had picked up a portfolio with drawings and she was selecting them, she put some of them aside, she passed her hands through Dragoş who was lying there motionless, she seemed not to see him, she passed the drawings through him as through air, she put some back in the portfolio, passing them through Dragoş again. I was silent. I felt like throwing up, a memory of a nightmare, I was wondering whether Maria knew and so had made that crazy selection on purpose.

When she realized that I was silent, Maria sighed and turned to me. "A few days ago," she said, "I met a boy, he said that he knew you . . ."

Then she took her drawings and left.

*While performing the leading role in Verdi's *I Vespri Siciliani* in Paris, the opera singer Martina Arroyo collapsed on stage in the second act because of a sudden drop in blood pressure. The singer Renata Scotto was asked to replace her. After agreeing, she announced that she would be unavailable for two weeks. The singer Montserrat Caballé was then appealed to, but she was ill. According to *Le Monde,* there are only three or four opera singers in the world able to perform the difficult part of Elena, and three of them are ill at the same time, one in Paris, the second in Milan, and the third in Turin.

21. Naturally, that evening I told Zenobia, in minute detail, of Maria's visit, I repeated to her all the words that we'd uttered, all that I was thinking during those moments, I even evoked the visitor's overwhelming moist warmth.

Zenobia was tired, she had worked a lot that day, she stood on a chair and caressed the bouquet of roses Maria had brought.

"There are twelve," she said.

"How can you be that calm?" I asked her, because the requital was starting. "From what I've told you it turns out that Dragoş doesn't exist there on the table, and you, instead of saying something, let me torment myself."

"I'm tired," said Zenobia, and she continued to caress the roses.

"You never help me," I said, "you always let me torment myself . . . Don't you realize? If Maria can't see him, if she can pass her hands and drawings through him, that means that I'm hallucinating and, what's worse, I'm connecting those hallucinations, I'm systematizing them . . ."

I knew I was talking nonsense, it was all the same to me, the system tacked together unwittingly for some time now annihilated itself in Zenobia's silence, I felt again how I was circled by that "other," which, to be borne, demanded short pauses of rational hysteria capable of burying it now and then in its desperate force; now my weakness and doubts persisted only by virtue of inertia.

And still, out of vanity, wishing in a way to show Zenobia that I was right, that the blame was hers and hers only, I walked toward Dragoş, I put my hand on his head, I felt his round forehead, his soft oily hair—they were there, under my fingers, he winked at me.

When I turned back to Zenobia, I saw that she wasn't caressing the roses anymore: from the bottom of each rose, where the flower meets the stem, she took out pins, so small and thin that you could barely see them.

"Look at this!" I marveled. "Maria claimed that they were picked in her garden . . ."

"Maybe they were," said Zenobia.

Then I remembered that this was, in fact, what some florists use to do when they wanted the carnations and rose blossoms to last longer . . .

*In just one year in the Republic of South Africa 12 pairs of Siamese twins were born. Professor Trevor Jenkins believes this is an extremely rare phenomenon that demands further study, since at most one pair of such twins is born worldwide every year.

22. One afternoon a little later, I was tired, I had some pohems in front of me, I sat with my cheek pressed against them, Zenobia wasn't home, I was on a very fine line between pohetry and the rest, which had to be dealt with carefully.

I could have dozed off or maybe I did, my head on the table: I had finished writing. It was, in a way, like when you start to die, anyway . . .

I sat with my head on the table, over my pohems, when the door opened slo-ow-ly, I thought it was Zenobia, and a child, three or four years old, delicate and pale, came into the room.

I don't know why, I thought that he could have been Empedocles as a child and I felt like laughing because those ancients, when they come, are always solemn, they wouldn't smile for anything in the world, and they are polite too (I had this experience with Empedocles before, he was all for giving me advice, I was looking at his bronze sandal with covetous eyes, the one left at the mouth of the volcano, I liked its style, I wanted to ask him if I could wear it for a few hours, I would have made all the boys on Leonida Street die of envy, the street where I lived back then with my mother and my four sisters, while Andrei, my older brother, wandered somewhere in the country; but Empedocles was pestering me: "You have to learn to think with your hands." I wanted to tell him to shut his smart little mouth because my hands had started to hurt from all this thinking . . .)

Then I thought that the little boy visiting me could be the child of one of my neighbors and that he came to us by accident, such things do happen, or not, at the same time, you can't possibly know if you don't know . . .

The little boy seemed not to see me, he didn't pay any attention to me, he was looking at Dragoş, I even thought of asking him, supposing that he was Empedocles, how on earth he had erred regarding the way of death; I wanted to chat with him on this subject but I was too sleepy, I could hardly keep my eyelids from drooping.

The child stood still in his loose-fitting little gown, a few steps from the table under the window; he kept his hands behind his back, he had leaned slightly forward, he watched attentively and didn't say a word.

Quite a few minutes passed in this way, I almost dozed off, when Dragoş jumped down from the table and started hopping around the child.

"Cut it out," I tried to stop him. "You'll frighten the child . . ."

But the words, like a kind of grumble, could hardly get out of my mouth. However, Dragoş understood them and stopped for a moment.

"He's not frightened," he told me. "He's my friend, he came to play . . ."

"Your friend, my ass," I managed to grumble while he resumed his dance around the child.

I saw and heard them as if from inside a cube of fog, the child's hands shone, but his face hadn't turned green yet, I was so sleepy I could have thrown myself from the chair directly between the bedsheets, as if into water; I could hardly crawl up to the sofa, I stumbled several times and then I stretched out on it facing them.

I don't know why, I persisted in keeping my eyes open, I could have seen them anyway, they had both started to dance, they hopped like crazy, they jumped through the air and chuckled, and then Dragoş stood on all fours, the child climbed on his back, they went around the room like this. When I managed to raise my eyelids more I saw them like some nebulous spots moving to and fro, and they completely ignored me, I wanted to shout to them to calm down and to let me sleep, my jaws were stuck, I only managed to utter some pitiful noises: "ob-ob-ob . . ."

Then they calmed down, I could see their faces clearly again, their faces looked strangely like mine, I didn't understand and I didn't even try to, how could that pitiful child and the senile old man with his fleecy goat face look so much like me, I felt that an indefinable communion existed between us, it was as if we were gamboling, all three of us, in the same refreshing water and I could have kicked all three of them for not letting me sleep.

Afterward Dragoş leisurely settled into my chair, at the small table where I wrote, he took one of my pohems, and then another and another, three in all, he made paper airplanes out of them, the child, silent and attentive, watched him and he too smoothed out their edges a little with his fingernail and launched them into the room.

I felt like howling and laughing, I couldn't have cared less about the pohems and myself, I found myself moving (inside) my fingers; I did (inside) exactly what Dragoş was doing; my right arm throbbed (inside): it launched the planes at the same time as the child's frail arm; there was an amazing similarity in our gestures (inside). Afterward I got bored, they stopped playing. Dragoş gestured as if saluting me, with his hand touching the fur cap, the child ignored me, and they both left the room slo-ow-ly, while I collapsed into a deep sleep.

By the time Zenobia returned, it had long been dark, she turned on the lights, she woke me up.

"What's the matter with you?" she asked. "Why are you moaning?"

I told her that maybe I was working too hard and so I'd had a pleasant and unpleasant nightmare, that a little boy had visited me. "Imagine," I said, "I believe that he was Empedocles as a child, a little boy, the thing is, he was my spitting image; now, don't think that I'm saying this out of vanity, he was a pitiful little boy; besides, that old fart Dragoş pulled the dirty trick of slinking off without saying good-bye to you, he also looked like the two of us . . ."

Zenobia sat on a chair to cry a little, maybe she was tired, maybe she was sorry because Dragoş had left us. Afterward she said "I'm through!" and stood up. I recounted the rest of what had happened. She listened to me while straightening up the house, like any other housewife. She bent down three times and picked some paper planes up from the floor, three in all, but she didn't put them next to the other pohems, she put them instead on the table that could have overlooked the swamps.

III

• ◻ ▪ ◻ •

THE CORRIDOR

1. YOU OPEN A DOOR AND THERE IS ANOTHER ONE, AND THEN another and another, until the last one, which doesn't even exist, and so on, until you find yourself at the first one, which doesn't even exist, and you take a stroll to old places because what you thought had released you, and really had released you, becomes a trap and brings you back there to finally understand that your last truth is just as illusory as the first one and to remember that you are always walking a fine line.

2. A few days after Dragoş's departure, I set off on foot, it couldn't have been far.

I sauntered, I stopped every now and then, I rested my forehead against the wall of a house and cried, I liked the trick; a little old man stopped to ask me why I was crying and whether I needed anything.

"Give me half of your handkerchief to put to honest use," I told him, shifting my forehead to his shoulders, "because I'm going to see my family, a widowed-and-maybe-at-the-point-of-death mother and an oligophrenic young woman, my older sister."

The little old man looked at me in terror, pulled back, and scurried away as fast as he could, even though I told him only true things.

It was a beautiful and necessary game, I wanted to balance myself; as usual, that morning too many things had happened, Zenobia had gone out and left me home alone and I had trodden on steps that were too hot, I felt the urge to cool my soles, to place them on common asphalt.

I cried, without reason, to relax, with my forehead against the wall of a house on Romană Street.

It was obvious that I was wasting my time: except for that compassionate little old man, nobody stopped to ask me what was the matter; that's why I sat on the curb, I babbled something, I followed the development of my thoughts; first an illustrious personage came to mind, I said to myself that any real poet knows more than all the volumes that that personage wrote about the depths of behings or at least about his own psychic entrails; then another one, "oh yes," I said to myself, "this one comes closer, unfortunately I have to bid him farewell on the steps of some cathedral"; then a third: why did he appear to me, because that *other of everyone* appeared only when I gestured to him, as now, with the gesture of someone wiping his nose or wiping the sweat from his forehead so that *he himself* could withstand the inner burn?

Then I saw Aunt Linica crossing to the other sidewalk, she had died long ago, but other equally dead people passed by, I had learned to recognize them; she waved to me and turned past Tunari School, "maybe she's going to visit Mother, maybe she's waiting for me," I said to myself, getting ready to go after her and ask some questions, for instance, whether she married again *over there,* whether the groom, supposing that he would be the same, stuck back on the legs that were cut off by the train on his way to his wedding, and so on.

Then I stood up and left, I had gotten bored, I turned past Tunari School on Leonida Street, I opened the rusty iron gate, which made a prolonged squeak, I walked along the narrow path in the yard (there was a lilac tree with three marks in white paint on its trunk), and I walked into the house without knocking.

I usually found my sister Zoe-Olga embroidering abstract shapes on small pieces of cloth in red cotton thread, I loved them madly; she didn't know how to read or write, I had just managed to teach her, when I was around seven and she was around nineteen, to draw four capital letters: O, L, G, A, but she would always add an E after them, so she signed herself OLGAE; not only that, she would listen with great interest to the concerts broadcast on the radio and enunciate with extreme precision the names of the most rarely heard musical instruments; now she was alone, I could freely discuss anything with her.

"Is Mother home?" I asked her.

"No, she's out on the streets," she answered.

"Dolly," I asked (that was the term of endearment that I used with her sometimes), "did Aunt Linica drop by?"

"She did a moment ago, just for a little while, because she died," she told me.

"And what did she say?"

"What could she say, the poor thing . . . ? She asked about you."

"Was I here?" I asked.

"No, you weren't, it was only her, she said you would come . . ."

"Go check the other room," I told her. "Maybe I was there."

"I'm going," she said obligingly.

She went to the next room, she returned a few moments later.

"You weren't there," she said.

"Then that means I'm here," I said.

"Yes," she confirmed.

I fell silent for a while, then I asked her again: "Besides Aunt Linica, did anybody else ask for me?"

"Yes, Constantin asked for you, he died too, he was wearing a jacket and a hat."

"If he comes again, tell him to look for me in the street. Will you remember that?"

"Yes."

"You'd better make a note, so you won't forget." (I gave her a scrap of paper and a pencil stub, she carefully drew a few hieroglyphs on it.) "When Mother gets home, tell her I'll come again, on her birthday, to bring her a present . . ."

"And what will you bring me when I die?"

"A bridal gown. Make a note of that too, so I won't forget."

She wrote a note, just as conscientiously, with the same hieroglyphs, adding the signature OLGAE, her eyes shone with joy, I stretched out on the divan, after a little while I fell asleep, it was nice there, on the divan, a pleasant breeze came in through the open windows, the thin curtains fluttered . . .

3. On my way home I thought of my friends, most of them scum, I had cared for some of them, I met them in my own way, that is, I wandered the streets until one of them appeared, he would come directly to me, he wouldn't have the slightest idea that I had called him, sometimes I thought of one in particular, it was all the same to me, I just wanted to see whom I would meet in that state (maybe I should disentangle a little the painful mechanisms of failures too, but I prefer to forget them); I had been practicing my meetings with particular people for a long time, since my adolescence when I languished over a small and miserable creature, I had found out her name but I didn't know where she lived, I would set off, I would turn to the left or to the right, I was guided by a kind of luminosity, when I saw her I wouldn't say a word, I hardly greeted her.

Everything had started with some extinguished matches tossed into a cold stove, I won't insist on it; then I would make appointments for those whom I would name "Princes of the Balkans" and they went by convinced that they were going to parades, moving like epileptic particles; and back then I liked going to a big sports stadium where I would settle in an hour before the arrival of the first people so I could see it filling up, while the people, convinced that each one of them took the seat that he himself had chosen, ignoring the terrible law of filling that was driving them in accordance with its necessities, drowned in the sad quantum waters of the whole.

In the course of time those exercises bored me; besides, in such matters, exaggeration and the exercise of force tempted me, please remember, only in moments of weakness and low self-confidence.

Perhaps I'm going through such a moment now, when I write (because it seems that I am writing) about this rubbish that, as a matter of fact, I don't give a damn about.

*In Baigorra (Argentina), in the roots of a tree uprooted by the storm, giant ants were discovered, about five times larger than normal ones.

4. So on my way home I was thinking of my friends before my departure for the swamps; Constantin had died and may his memory be everlasting, then he looked for me on Leonida Street, he had some business with me.

This caricature with a bird's head, a cross between a turkey's and a chicken's, with his nose like a soft bill hanging down over his mouth, this dirty dead man, small and weedy, his hair always plastered down, with clothes of an exemplary elegance, this perfect product of the zone of promiscuity that Nature hatches to balance itself and then vomits out, like a secret, under her other side, had appeared in my life at about the age of eighteen, maybe from the same need to balance, or maybe only because, through a strange coincidence, we both had the same last name.

Back then I probably had a surplus of energy that had to be expended and I played rugby twice a week, on Thursdays for training, on Sundays for the game, I was the youngest on the team, I played forward beautifully; after the game the boys would go drink beer, catch the streetcar, hold the back door open, spit on women's dresses, they would have a swell time and they would end up at night in a movie theater or who knows where, while I would visit a friend of mine, a woman lawyer much older than I (she was already twenty-four), a beauty whose hair was completely white, she would wipe my broken eyebrows or my scratched shoulder blades with alcohol, we would make love.

Once, on an autumn Sunday, in the showers after the game, Constantin appeared wearing a superb white jersey, I had seen him hanging around there before; Gică Wirth, who played the wing in the opposing team, said to him: "Hey, skinny, give me that jersey, I want to try it on."

Constantin took off his jersey and gave it to him, Gică Wirth polished his leather shoes with it, then threw it at Constantin's head, the others were laughing. Constantin seemed happy, I could have kicked him, because I am one of those people who cry at the movies even when I realize that I should have died laughing, but I took pity on him, he was too distressing, I said nothing, I minded my own business.

As I left, I found him next to me. He was smiling.

"Where do you live?" he asked me.

"What do you care?" I answered him.

"Wait, let me tell you," he said, "I've known you for a long time, and I have your photo on a page of a newspaper showing pupils who've been awarded prizes, you were little, my picture is next to yours, I was awarded a prize too, I saved it because we both have the same last name, if you don't have it, I can give it to you, I'll cut it out of the newspaper with scissors and give it to you."

"I live at 5 Leonida," I told him, "bring the photo tonight

because I don't have it, but why are you so miserable, how on earth can you stand those guys making fun of you?"

"I stand it because I'm ugly," he said, "it's easy for you because you're handsome, but I love a woman, I'm mad about her and she doesn't like me, I watch you to imitate you, to impress her; besides, I spend all I have on clothes; every now and then, when I save up two or three months' pay, don't ask me how, I go visit her, she thinks I'm flush, the bad part is that every time I come back from her I have an illness and I have to wait until I get well, then I go see her again, otherwise I'd die."

"I like you," I told him. "And now beat it. Stop by tonight, if I'm not home leave the picture, we'll talk some other time, I'm busy now . . ."

That night, around eight, Constantin came by with the photo, I wasn't home, he left it there for me, it was a yellowed clipping from *The Morning* newspaper, I tore it up, it showed a child wearing a miserable little vest, the child had a crown of flowers on his right arm and he looked rather askance at the world, that was me.

5. About that time I moved out and lived alone for a while on a rather long corridor that I would only run and never walk through, a dark and sordid corridor, to the right, as you came in, was the line of the servants' rooms (they were women who came from remote places in the mountains, I would hear them in the morning telling each other in their native dialect their dreams populated by black bulls that thrust their horns through the windows of the rooms on the eighth or ninth floor, I don't remember anymore), to the left there was the communal shower, used mainly on Saturdays, the communal toilet, and the communal sink, plus the room of a young painter, he grew a beard, he prayed with the door wide open, in order to be seen (but the women from the mountains were not so easily fooled, they would

spit and cross themselves behind his back), he had a lover, a schoolgirl, she visited him during classes, she brought him food in her knapsack, he beat her to a pulp and so on, there was an amorous drama going on.

I forgot to mention that at the end of that corridor on the highest floor of a high-rise building on Moşilor Way at Domniţei Boulevard, I lived in a small room and was visited by beings with luminous hands and transparent faces, I won't say too much about them; had they not left palpable traces, I would have believed that I had visions, we would talk for hours, once, for instance, they brought me a sack of potatoes, they emptied it in the middle of the room, for a long time I ate nothing but boiled potatoes, without salt, they were good, if anyone asked why those potatoes were in the middle of the room, I would say, for instance, that a cousin of mine sent them from the country, from the Prahova district, and no one would be surprised.

I ate eggplant back then, please remember this detail, a vegetable in no way commendable, I had a round balcony with a spider of wire hanging from the ceiling, I would slice the eggplant, hang it on a string next to the spider, where it dried, I would put some water on the stove, enough for this purpose, wait until the water boiled, take the sliced eggplant, dry and light as air, I would put it in the boiling water, leave it to boil for ten or fifteen minutes, and then I ate it, without salt, it wasn't good; on the same balcony I used to dry the leaves that I smoked in my pipe, I tried all kinds of leaves, nothing but quince leaves could be used for this purpose, although even they had the disadvantage of leaving a black and unpleasant oil in my pipe, that's why I eventually tried to find tobacco.

In giving you these recipes, useful under certain circumstances, I wouldn't like to leave the impression that I was poor, although I didn't possess even a shirt on my back, I didn't look bad, although I lacked tobacco, which was more unpleasant; I never had the feeling of poverty, I wasn't interested in such stuff, furthermore, I was a little snobbish because my only glass, which I used for drinking from the communal sink, was of Baccarat crystal, and my only plate, which I used for eating my eggplant and potatoes, without salt, please remember this unimportant detail, had on its back the mark of the finest English porcelain.

*Plato's famous olive tree was replanted in the same spot after being uprooted by a bus. Specialists confirmed that the olive tree is more than 2500 years old.

6. On that corridor there was an aging bride who was lying in wait for me, a Viennese lady about forty-two years old, her hair beautifully bleached, the door of her room was toward the end of the corridor, next to and off to the side of the door to my room, the lady lived with her mother, whose moans of a veteran of suffering I would hear night and day, maybe I exaggerate when I say that she was lying in wait for me, it could have been *simple coincidence* but almost every morning, when I would go to buy bread or eggplant, that lady (her name was approximately Gerda) would come out to greet me.

In her right hand she would hold a pot, in her left hand a clove of garlic.

"See how vehy clean I am?" she would say every time (she meant to say "very" but she would constantly drop her *r*'s). "See how vehy clean I am? I even wash the gahlic which shouldn't need washing because it is covehed by its peel but I still wash it."

"Madam," I would say to her, while she poured the nocturnal liquids from the pot into the communal sink, "I properly appreciate this hygienic action, the more so since I myself couldn't say that I'm clean, although I'm pure," and so on, polite things.

One morning, after again drawing my attention to the fact that she was extraordinarily clean, Mrs. Gerda added:

"Hemembeh that I am like a sisteh whom you can thust, although I am upset with you because I saw you yestehday bahefoot on the stheet; why wehe you bahefoot?"

"Madam," I told her, "these morning discussions, here, in the corridor, ennoble me, that's why I'm going to explain this to you: I had taken my sandals to be repaired."

"Well, well," she said, "but yesterday you also left the dooh open and you wehe naked, why do you stay naked with the dooh open, it's not phopeh."

"I was reading a book, madam, by one Kierkegaard, I can lend it to you if you want."

"Thank you," she said, "hight now I'm heading anotheh novel."

And after she poured the contents of the pot into the sink and rinsed the garlic in a demonstrative way, Mrs. Gerda turned to me and whispered as if telling a secret: "I heahd that you also white . . ."

"Yes, madam," I confessed to her, "I write till I can't go on."

"What do you white?" she asked me, "and why do you white?"

"It's an infirmity, madam, a birth defect, it seizes me, just like that," I said. "I have my own feelings, and I feel like crying every time I talk about this, I can't explain verbally, if you would lend me the pot for an instant I would cry in it as if it were a lachrymatory and maybe you would understand me . . ."

"You can khy," she told me, "I am like a sisteh to you," and she handed me the pot.

I took it and I cried in it, because it was necessary, it was one of those situations, anyway, I used the pot, it was a way of expressing myself and my tears fell drop, drop, I had floated all night long in sublime circles, I wanted to escape from the memory of a too painful serenity, I cried like a baby, I felt like I would die laughing, I was telling myself:

"You cretin, go buy eggplant or take a walk in the street, or, what the hell, go to a movie."

"Does it huht?" Mrs. Gerda asked me, concerned.

"Yes it does, Mrs. Gerda, what do you think? I fall into a kind of trance, a kind of happiness more difficult to bear than pain. Then I'm tortured by only one fear, pleasant and terrible: not to be pulverized, I can tell you, you are like a sister, then I float (don't be afraid) and, here you go, the pot, I wasn't able to fill it up but I'm all right now, I'm going to buy eggplant and bread . . ."

"You should see a doctoh," Mrs. Gerda said to me, "I can take you if you want . . ."

"You are too kind, Mrs. Gerda; with the innocence that you possess, in spite of your age (I consider you, of course, a virgin, and please don't misunderstand me) you should have, like the Phoenician angels, three pairs of wings: one to cover your face, one to cover your legs, and one to fly. Then, if you'd give me permission, I would establish my household on your shoulder bones and maybe I would go see a doctor too."

"I still think that you ahe sick," Mrs. Gerda told me, as she returned with dignity to her room.

7. After that, I was deaf for a while, it was extraordinary, I couldn't hear a thing, I was stopped up with solid earwax, I was like a bottle filled with the pure and free simplicity of my situation, I would point to my ear: "I'm deaf, what do you think about that!" I had an innocent smile, the others were understanding, some even sympathized with me although they looked glad that they could hear, I had escaped, they could distinguish themselves as much as they wanted in their mosaic of already drawn-up questions and answers, they could theorize their theories by themselves as much as they wanted in order to chop their sonorous cabbage amid the sweet joys of training.

The bad part is that one day, pop! my earwax cracked and I started to hear again, I could have stopped speaking instead and made myself mute, but that seemed weird to me, it would have been unfair, and then, however mute you are, you still can hear the words, they sneak unhindered through your marrow, so I just minded my own business.

8. Once, long ago, I was in a cornfield, near fall, the corn had dried out; in the middle of the field there was a black-smith's shed and, a few steps away, a little house, some kind of hut with a thatched roof, I was sitting next to the black-smith, he was working on a red-hot horseshoe, between the hammer blows I could hear the corn rustling.

Then, from the house, Bach in person started to play, he played the dulcimer, he was improvising, I don't know if you've ever heard Bach playing in a shed in a dry cornfield, improvising at the dulcimer, the sounds spread like smoke, they pervaded the sky, they made me dizzy.

"Who's playing?" I asked the blacksmith.

"That's my son-in-law," he answered, "at night he plays in a tavern in Bucharest, now he's practicing . . ."

After a while the music fell silent and Bach appeared in striped pajamas in the doorway of the hut, he was younger, he looked livid, ecstasy had dimmed his eyes, he was totter-ing, drunk on music, I regretted his silence, I would have liked to have heard his words, to have heard what can be said in that state; then a little girl, two or three years old, his daughter, rushed from the cornfield, she stumbled and fell at his feet and Bach, from beyond dreams, from the dizzi-ness of harmonies, said to her: "When I let you have it, you'll s—— in your pants again . . ."

Those were the words.

9. While I evoke, standing, like that Bach, on the threshold, I have the feeling that I've begun to perpetrate a nohvel and this I abhor; anyway, writing like an unfortunate prose

writer about this and that I only reconstitute the corridor that I used to run through, the rest isn't at all important; and that corridor can't be reconstituted differently when at one end the visions liquefy you and at the other end you go to buy eggplant and so on, while in its middle Mrs. Gerda waits for you with her customary pot; there is, perhaps, a filter zone and through it passes only what by nature can pass regardless of receptiveness or conscious criteria, a hard zone that can be penetrated only by what is destined to become conveyable, a zone whose wild perfection is surpassed only by the necessity (which is equally wild) of remaining in it for a while.

If you pass a fraction of an inch higher, something else happens (at first I would even get scared), if you pass a fraction of an inch lower, pitiful texts are born, it's as though you began sifting the salt from the waters of an immense ocean. But what am I rambling on about, what am I explaining? Anyway . . .

*The population of Saint Pierre and Miquelon, a group of islands situated in the west of the Atlantic Ocean, has been witnessing for some days now, without being able to intervene, the death throes of 63 cetaceans known by the name of *Steno rostratus,* stranded on the empty beaches of the archipelago.

10. So at the time when I ran insulted and disgusted down the corridor, I floated all night long and it seems that I grumbled too loudly because the next day, greeting me at the sink, after having reminded me how clean she was and having noticed the bandage that covered my right fist, Mrs. Gerda said:

"Wehe you sick last night?"

"No. Why?"

"Because I heahd you talking to youhself, I thought you wehe delihious."

"I wasn't delirious, Mrs. Gerda, I think I talked in my sleep."

"It's impossible," said Mrs. Gerda, "you wehen't sleeping, you banged against the walls, I heahd you."

"It's possible, Mrs. Gerda, that I banged against the walls in my sleep; I ask you not to tell anybody, because I'm a somnambulist too, and I get insomnia . . ."

"I know how to keep a sekhet," Mrs. Gerda assured me. "I get insomnia too, even though I am not a somnambulist, but if this happens to you again, knock on the wall, we could go out into the cohhidoh and have a talk . . ."

"You are extraordinarily kind, Mrs. Gerda, I have to admit, but I'm afraid we wouldn't have anything to talk about, at night, the two of us, not in the corridor or anywhere else, because, you know, when I'm in a state like last night I don't use words in discussions, I am content with letters and then, when it comes to a word in Romanian, a language we have both mastered perfectly, I feel like, I don't know why, using only one letter of that word, and even that one translated into a foreign language . . ."

"You ahen't fevehish, by any chance?" Mrs. Gerda asked.

"I could be, Mrs. Gerda, and why not? But what I'm telling you is nothing but the truth, sometimes I'm in a state from which I want to communicate something and then bang! the words come and that state, if I don't get carried away by them, goes to hell and only then do you like it because you start to recognize in my words something well known to you, whereas I, since I was born, have had this idea that I have to communicate forgotten truths from some place where my sensitivity could meet the great general sensitivity lost on the way, I ask you to excuse me for using the word sensitivity, I feel like crying with sorrow because the point in question is completely different, but you see how I am and there's nothing I can do, in this way you can also appreciate, more or less, or at least you can prefigure, I know that you are cultivated, you proved it to me by confiding to me the fact that you read nohvels, but literature is not the point nor are words, I couldn't care less about literature and words, that's why I wouldn't use the word sensitivity or any other stupidity because now a word in Kurdish or another language comes to me, who the hell knows where it comes from but it does, and other times only one letter of it or its initial comes to me (take, for instance, the letter *U*: when it is in Gothic script it abbreviates, purifies, and expresses for me, I beg your pardon, *the Unknown,* I think that it is related to *Unbekannt,* do you see the relation? do you see where the damned word comes from?), and for you who are, even though you haven't confided it, I feel that you are very musically inclined too, it's like when you go to the opera and, instead of dashing off before the overture starts, you sit nervously in a chair and can hardly wait for that aria that you know by heart (*a-a-di-i-o del pa-ssa-a-to!*), and when the aria comes you hum along ultrasatisfied because you know it, and you don't know that exactly what you know prevents you from knowing, while I beg your pardon for this idiot litany and I admire you for your patience in listening to me, amen."

"I am suhe, howeveh, that you ahe fevehish, maybe fhom this bandaged fist, let me see," said Mrs. Gerda.

And putting down the pot, she touched my cheeks with her very caressive fingers.

"Take your hand off me!" I shouted so loudly that from the other end of the corridor the echo answered: "Off me . . ."

"Oh deah!" said Mrs. Gerda, amazed by my unexpected rudeness. "But I'm like a sisteh to you . . ."

"I've seen many sisters like you, Mrs. Gerda, there was one, for example, Mrs. Ojog, who was your current age when I had just turned fourteen, she had come from America, she smoked cigars, she played poker with Mother, she had a little dog, Buster, a filthy cur with no hair; once, in the evening, after the poker game, she said that she didn't like going home alone in the streets, Mother said that it was all right, Gellu could walk you home, I walked her home, while we were walking she talked about various things, Buster wagged his little tail, he walked behind us, you would've said that he rubbed his little paws with delight that the business was turning out well, at the gate Mrs. Ojog said: 'I'd like to ask you inside to give you a good cigarette, I know that you are a passionate smoker, don't pretend now, you don't need to, you can trust me because I consider you mature and I'm like a sister to you, but my husband is out of town and what would the neighbors say?' I mumbled something, I don't know what, and when I ran from her bed I don't remember how I got home, all the time I kept thinking that she was a friend of Mother's, when she came to visit us I would hide, I was ashamed, until one day, pop! the shame went away by itself, maybe because on that day Mother said that I could play too for a little while in her place, while she fixed coffee, that she would give me money for the game (but I had to return it eventually, so I wouldn't get used to money), they played for small stakes, just for fun; then I settled into the chair, facing Mrs. Ojog, and while playing I pissed under the table on Mrs. Ojog's skirt, I could have died laughing; when they, Mrs. Ojog and the others, realized what was happening they flared up, Mother said: 'He's crazy,' and so on, I believe that she rejoiced in her heart . . ."

"Oh deah!" said Mrs. Gerda. "You ahe indecent . . ."

"You're stupid," I said. "How am I indecent? These things are too complicated for your pot, that's why they appear indecent to you, that's their appearance, as the appearance of apparent things is to appear decent, listen to me; look, I'll give you an example, let me tell you something that happened to me just yesterday and, if your mind works at all, you'll understand why I remembered Mrs. Ojog and Buster particularly now, after the sublime moments of last night; so yesterday I walked down the street freshly shaven, without a bandage on my hand, and with clean socks, and a young woman followed me down the street for about an hour.

"I never follow young ladies on the street, I'm not in the habit. But I liked it, I was thinking of one Turcu, an upholsterer on Vasile Lascăr Street, who wears a lavaliere and has long hair, you would swear that he's at least Novalis even though he's about forty and short and squat, but that doesn't matter, young ladies follow him and ask for autographs, they think he's a poet, while my hair is cut short or not cut at all and so nobody asks for autographs, sometimes I bear a grudge against Turcu, so yesterday, when that young woman followed me I was extremely happy, I thought: Look, since it seems she swallowed the bait several times with Turcu and has learned the lesson, now she knows who's a pohet and who's not, wait, she's a fan, no doubt about it, and she knows by heart at least my last unpublished pohem entitled 'Gheorghe Lazăr's Boots' or a few lines from another pohem of mine, likewise unpublished, such as 'because my woman doesn't rain' or 'locusts are the most Constantin,' I expected her to recite them and then tell me: 'Recite something else if you can!' I had already stopped beside a wall, honestly that was a comfort for my flayed being, and I stared into the void, more in profile, when she took heart and held out a fountain pen and a piece of paper and asked me, in English, for an autograph.

"Then my receptiveness started to work, a suspicion arose in my mind, I punched the wall on which I had leaned, I punched it so hard that I hurt my fist and I asked her: 'What for?'

"She was a little scared because blood was dripping from my fist and she asked me whether I was one Buster Crabbe, a film actor who played Tarzan and was my spitting image, she said; she had just seen my photo in a special-interest magazine where she had read that Buster Crabbe was in Bucharest and she had thought . . .

"Then I told her that Buster Crabbe wasn't worth a damn compared with one Buster Ojog that I had met some years before and who perhaps resembled me even though he was always wagging his little tail, I hoped he had croaked in the meantime because life is, fortunately, short but you realize my state of mind, and so on, wait . . ."

But Mrs. Gerda didn't wait and ran into her room where, amid the moans of her ailing old mother, I heard her locking the door.

11. Now, when you review, you might get the impression that I talk rather too much and too rudely about inessential matters; and you might be annoyed by the dimensions acquired by a Mrs. Gerda or others like her, dimensions otherwise not at all negligible for my existence; you might even put this down to my intention to obscure what was happening on the other side, at the other end of the corridor for instance, where the surface ceased to exist as such, anyway, and where I considered myself, for example, the hub of the universe, an essential and miserable hub, I won't insist on it.

This way one might end up with a character who wasn't me and a corridor in which I never wandered; anyway, ignoring my *innée* gentleness and the surrounding stenches of existence, a rather rude boy could appear in my place, which is absolutely all the same to me, while I, on this cold October day when I write, will leave the room and the boring ritual of evocation for a while and, driven by a real human necessity, will head toward the end of the yard where a bird recently arrived from the earth's north will smile at my purity and bring me news about a realm without up and down.

*The Widzel scientific research base in the extreme north of Sweden was subjected to a siege by about 30 polar bears. They kept the researchers, who wouldn't dare leave the base after nightfall, under strict surveillance. It seems that the animals wanted to regain their old rights in this area, which constituted one of their favorite territories, forcing the researchers to go somewhere else.

12. Also about the time of the corridor I had to live for approximately ten days in another forest, I had been given a horse, I watered him with a canvas bucket from the spring in the immediate vicinity, I curried him, I fed him from a sack of oats, I slept next to him, it was cold at night, many times I would wake up with my head resting on the warm heap of dung, I ate the little food that I had, all this happened within an area of four square yards, beyond which death lay in wait for me.

I sat there on the layer of wet leaves formed by the years, it rained sometimes, I would pull the smelly blanket from under the saddle over my head, one day I started to rummage in the layer under me, to move the rotten leaves aside; beginning at a depth of about eight inches the leaves eaten by time and dampness started to look like lace, embroidery, and filigree, I would lift them with two fingers toward the yellowish light filtered through the branches of the trees and I would look at them for minutes at a time, they rewarded me for my lamentable existence, within that area of four square yards at whose limit death was lying in wait for me was the miracle. All it took was digging . . .

13. At the time of the corridor I would sometimes visit one of my friends too, I would knock at his door, go inside, circle the table, and leave immediately or stay; if I happened to stay, how beautifully we talked about the terrible curses that cause pohetry to crumble or about I don't know what, while pohetry continued to crumble in its perfectly set-in-order curses uttered by other, more experienced monsters; at other times, if I was tired, I would lie on a couch there and I would sleep until I was awakened by the whispers of my friend who was, for example, still discoursing on the miseries of pohetry, then I would shout from the couch: "Shut *up*!" and my friend would stop, he felt that I terrorized him.

Naturally, I visited young ladies too, I won't insist on it,

I'll only say that at Maria's studio I passed decent hours, I would soliloquize about anything at all in front of her, about how bad this world is, about love and freedom, I would often remember the motto stitched on Marat's vest: *"Vivre libre ou mourir!"* I liked to talk in front of her, I was polite and gentle, I wouldn't even kiss her, she would be silent and sigh, I should have cried, I think that she would have comforted me; that woman lawyer had gone to Moldova for good, I walked her to the railroad station like a hero, we hugged good-bye, she said: "Take care of yourself," I smiled, for a long time my heart had been frozen, for a very long time, soon a young woman invited me to her place, a terrific villa, her parents weren't home, when I kissed her, her face reddened, her lips dried up, they shriveled as if from fever, so much so that I ran out of that place, and so on.

Then another evening, as I crossed Icon Garden on my way home and I felt wet and sad like a dog thrown in a ditch, I came across one of my cousins (he died later in an explosion, only his boots were recovered), on that autumn evening he sat on a bench beside his lover, he tried to persuade her to get down to it, she stubbornly refused, I was tired and cold, I sat on the bench next to them, my cousin introduced the young woman to me, that was his business, she said that she was glad, that she knew me by sight, I said good for her, I thought about going, about leaving them alone, my cousin was still trying to persuade her, they bored me, I was cold, I told that young woman to come make love with me and she came along.

14. By enumerating those vile little deeds that are part of almost every adolescent's life, I'm actually talking about a bed made with lily petals up to which the road leads among moldy residues and excrement; perhaps their purpose is to attenuate to a bearable level some scorching inner rays, perhaps my prattle feeds the prefigured force of everyone's

silence, and reveals inversely the other side where measures, all measures, are illusory, and so on . . .

Besides, when you're serene and calm you can hear from there the world's moans and then a pohem or painting with little flowers is perpetrated, because, as I said, only what can and must traverse intelligent plains comes through.

*The Court of Bentong (Malaysia) was forced to interrupt its activity for several days because of an invasion of caterpillars that literally occupied the whole building, crawling on walls, ceilings, and doors, covering the floors and all the furniture. It took several days to remove the millions of caterpillars.

15. At about the same time I lived, temporarily, in a village on the bank of the Someş, I was terribly sick, I crawled through the streets of the village by hanging on fences, I ate nothing but potatoes without salt, nothing else, please keep this detail in mind, I didn't talk to anybody, the locals stared at me as if I were a ghost.

A few weeks later, when I started to recover, a young woman from the Department of Classical Philology at the University of Bucharest came to see me, she cared about me, she found me ultrascrawny, my belly swollen by the potatoes, we went out for a walk, in the field, among daisies and poppies, to the grass so green that it seemed wet, we discussed different things, mostly classical matters, she had brought some books for me to read, I could hardly stand on my feet but I made conversation like an intelligent and cocksure person, I expressed my opinions regarding Theodore of Cyrenaica, called "the Atheist" and later "the God," and regarding Hipparchia of Maro, I even had some reservations, I was saddened by some details of their lives, lapses of behavior, pay attention; that's how it is when you discover the virtues of saliva, the young woman wasn't to be blamed at all.

And it so happened that suddenly the gases caused by my purifying but unbalanced diet started to put pressure on my bladder; I felt that I would die, that I would go mad with shame, there were two possible solutions: one consisted of the urgent evacuation of the bladder's liquid, the other, involving sound, related to the equally urgent dispersing of the gases, both solutions inconceivable in front of a girl from the Department of Classical Philology.

Soon I felt that I could not contain myself anymore, I threw myself face down on the earth, I beat the grass with my fists, I groaned as loudly as I could because I had chosen the infamous and degrading sonic solution, which could not be covered by my groans; the young woman looked at me dumbfounded, she was frightened.

"Make no mistake," I shouted, "when I talk about Theodore I have in mind only his way of life and I refer only to states, not ideas; don't put me in his or anybody else's category of people, don't put me any category whatsoever, don't forget this," I shouted (uselessly, because I couldn't conceal everything), "don't put labels on me, I'll suffocate, if I utter a name from those miserable books that you're bringing me, you'll immediately find a label for me; remember that I read to recognize not to cognize; remember that I don't live *pro* and *con,* like in your trap" (I shouted more and more furiously). "Remember that I am *outside,* and get out of here, and make it quick; go to the railroad station, leave me—"

The young woman tried to help me, she didn't know how, but I soon finished and we continued our walk as if nothing had happened, and I even think that she found enjoyable those hours spent with a pohet, on a field of daisies and poppies.

16. The techniques had escaped, they went mad in a chaotic chase; we multiplied like mad, there has never been a more wild and wonderful century; God! (this is an expression as good as any other) and what still awaits us! It seems that it

has just begun, although we live under an auspicious number; maybe there was a kind of miscounting and it'll be discovered that there are too many of us; there is a blade of grass that grew in only one night under the light of a star, it could tell us but no one would believe it, a frail and tiny blade of grass under the light of a barely visible star; no one would believe it because everyone knows so many things and all together we know even more, even I used to read one volume after another, I studied with much seriousness and great disgust, I passed examinations too, I was asked, whether in logic or in another god-awful subject, about Hegel, the boys said that I was in luck, as chance would have it, I could have just crammed Hegel and nothing else, I had my method, let me explain: I would close my eyes lightly, I would see the pages as if they were in front of me, exactly the way they were printed, down to the tiniest annotations, nothing escaped me, I would read them, I would enumerate everything faultlessly, I would repeat the entire litany, which I then tried to forget as soon as possible, to remain clean.

They wanted only to ascertain whether they had shoved me into the machinery; I felt like screaming, I had a brain too, as miserable as you like, it did what it could, among other things it was the author of my errors too, and they forced me to wrap my brain up in their moth-eaten sock while it growled like a dog that I carried in my skull.

*In western Kentucky a vigorous attack was launched against millions of blackbirds and thrushes by helicopters that sprayed detergents to dissolve the fats that impregnate the feathers of these birds. The birds can't survive in bad weather without this protection.

17. Like tectonic plates—massive, unconscious, and invisible—the forces were in movement; it was difficult to follow them on your poor little legs without slipping; it was difficult to stand still before the disproportion between them and you, to bring your condition into accord with its own

ferocious foundations; it so happened that sometimes I fell down for a while; a couple of times, for example, I was forced into an institutional room where I stayed, truth to tell, not too long, among honest thieves, there was a tub there too, in which, in the name of hygiene, we relieved ourselves and which we took turns emptying, but we couldn't sleep because only people with special qualities can sleep standing up and I didn't have anything to lean on to sleep; lice swarmed on the walls. When I succeeded in dozing off a little, squatting or crouching somewhere on the moldy cement, a man, a naked one, came in; they said he was crazy, anyway he was crazy by profession, which is almost the same thing, and he smeared my face with materials taken from the tub while the thieves laughed, they were having a little fun, the wretches; then came Mother, she ran from one office to another, she tried to save me, she had only one argument: "Don't you see? He's crazy! Instead of being like other boys his age, he's crazy . . ."

And since I was crazy, I would perform a little miracle, I would hold my fingers in a particular way or who knows what I would do, anyway, I was seized by an ample stillness, a vast serenity, the thieves calmed down, they started dozing as if on command, the naked fellow left me alone, the iron gate opened, I was asked outside, led to an office where I saw Mother, as if through a fog, talking to someone, a father of a family, naturally, who said: "It's a pity about this boy because he doesn't look stupid, but you don't know how to raise him . . . If he were mine I would beat him to within an inch of his life, I would bring him to his senses."

Mother continued her argumentation: "He's crazy, sir . . . He's crazy, I'm telling you . . ."

This happened to me twice, and every time, as I made my way home, being therefore, so to speak, free, distrust slipped in under my immense inner quietness; every time I asked myself the same question: had I really unlocked the gate by making that gesture or had I only foreseen that it would open?

18. But as the known is always more reassuring than the unknown, I tried to maintain the receptiveness of extremes like a gate that would lose its usefulness were it to close or open in only one direction; those apparently disorderly passages, actually containing the rigor of balance, lent my gestures and speech a tint of humor that transformed my writhings into grins; actually, in spite of explanations that poked their noses into everything manifesting an at least mental anemia, the apparent disorder of my states marked not only a possible pohetic technique but also the compensatory rigor of living free, of an order in motion, issuing again from its own meanders.

In order to maintain in relation to myself, in my moments of weakness, the factual truth of my states, I used the simplest methods possible, for example I played a game of solitaire, a well-known one, you put all the cards face up on the table by sevens, you are entitled to three more free spaces, in reserve, for moves in decreasing order, on the inverse color, and so on; usually, the game was won at the first try; at those moments I would say: "Let me see whether I can deal all aces in a row." I would shuffle the cards well and the damned aces would line up in a row.

Such an unimportant thing can appear as humor, even cheap humor, especially if one takes into account the existential gravity of the zone for which it has to serve as proof, but think of it: there were fifty-two well-shuffled cards and the aces lay down one after another (sometimes they didn't want to, and then I would grumble something and that would do it). Yet such unimportant things happened exactly the same way when applied to objects in general and to people too; I would clearly see to what extent the objects or the people were in connection with my states, I would acknowledge the at least unconscious power of objects and people to answer those states (sometimes obviously against them), I had to accept the idea, initially frightening, that the state of affairs was different and I tried not to disturb the law, to keep myself receptive to its movements, I don't know how to express it because the point in question doesn't need explanations, and so on.

Then the universes moved slowly and rocked me as they did when I was five or six years old and when at dusk, tired after play, I was flooded by an immense serenity, perhaps I was in paradise.

I usually recovered my senses with difficulty and I went out among people with paradise on my head like a fur cap, my vision was hazy, I would meet one of my friends, I would talk rather inconsiderately despite myself, I would forget to say "excuse me," and he would, with good reason, feel hurt and say, "This fellow is putting on airs," while I, because I didn't have a pot at hand, wanted to ask him to lend me his cap to cry in, that would have been, anyway, a situation . . .

*In Cagliari (Italy) an investigation is trying to determine why a family with 11 children withdrew into the mountains 15 years ago to live in a cave. Fifty-three-year-old Salvatore Cossu descends alone from time to time to the neighboring villages but he forbids the rest of his family to make this trip.

19. Back then, just before leaving for the swamps, I started to foresee Zenobia's existence (I didn't know her yet, I didn't even know what her name would be), she would come veiled among the other visitors who populated the room on the corridor, she would say nothing, the others withdrew, I couldn't see her face, I couldn't distinguish her features, she would wrap me in her warmth, I called her Isis or some other name, it doesn't matter.

When I began to stray she would disappear, it was difficult for me because I would remain alone in the waters that

I had muddied, my insufficiently prepared eyes would burn, I talk about something else because people don't really share this kind of thing with others and they're right not to do so, as they don't really talk among themselves about death and that's their business.

Back then I had the naïveté to write some kind of book about my invocations and Zenobia's apparitions that was strewn here and there with little theories; anyway, it was doomed to fail from the very start, maybe that's even why I wrote it; in spite of some pleasurable litherary fragments and some culthural judgments, the essential refused to let itself be expressed otherwise than by simple facts that appeared, as is their wont, rather far-fetched, just as they appear even now, what can I do . . .

I mention those notations, which I wouldn't feel capable of rereading, only because, among many other omissions, voluntary or not, I have the impression that they also contain a sort of invocation customary to myself that I transcribe only now:

20. let me not forget in the first place the hat i had procured a; black hat with a wide and sagging brim like a poet wore in a czechoslovakian play a shitty one where eve rything happened in a basement room; i also had a suit some velvet it covered me well in it i
felt like a basketball player of adequate height
i walked to and fro on my hind legs on my toes like a
trained dog
i walked on my toes with my little paws bent at the joints
with;
my head stuck tight to my neck with my eyes rolled
in a park; Isis was beside me she loved me; others gathered
by twos by threes to sing i recited alone having only
one fan but when i saw girls i would walk on my toes and
recite
Isis said nothing she knew that it wasn't possible otherwise i

saw two or three girls i started to walk with; the hat
on my head but much more desperate i recited as loudly as
i could
the girls passed by with some boys who appreciated me
i walked much more desperately one girl said: "don't shout
like that because
you look like a tramp" she was scared by my walk and my
black hat
she wanted to make me sad to make me die of embarrassment with my hat and all
i was madly courageous i recited: "maybe i am and so what
if i am?" she liked it i felt that she was beginning to like me
i was
desperate i improvised at random i was; miserable with that
hat i
deafened myself reciting i walked; on my toes around the
girls they
were beginning to like me i recited:
"you just say that about me it's easy for you because i'm a
miserable white
the last white of this millennium which is the last while;
you are pink green and blue the last; white of the millennium
i walk like a trained dog it's easy for you because etc etc"

i shouted loudly i improvised about the miserable white
that contains
all kinds of things plus the desperation of the end that coin-
cides with their
last calculations about; the fate of the last white retained
on their plantations i walked with my eyes bulging under
my black hat the girls were beginning to like me i reached
an alley with
tall trees Isis bent and; whispered in my ear:
"don't recite anymore; Cantor the mathematician walks
around here and he eats you

a mathematician is something at that damned church he
sings there but
this one is; a mean and vengeful one a kind of exterminat-
ing angel"
i was madly courageous the girls were beginning to like me
i shouted at Him
"it's easy for you to eat me because i am the last white but
just so you know
i don't care and i'll recite"; (He didn't appear He was
in the church i didn't see Him) i turned to follow the girls i
recited; scar
ed i walked on my toes the girls descended toward a sluice
paved with silvery slabs i; made a detour behind the trees
"don't recite anymore" said Isis "there's a professional
around here you're
making a fool of yourself"
"i couldn't care less for the mother of all professionals" i said
"it's easy
for them but i; am the last white on this stinking planet"
actually i recited tragic matters i can't express them because
they are
rather unclear i followed the girls to the sluice on the slabs
near the watchman's booth the door; was open
in front of it was an armoire with the panels of cheap gl; ass
then the watchman came out (halfway only) with a hammer
in his hand he wanted to hit me on the fingers so i wouldn't
look
but he; retreated immediately because the girls had gotten
scared
and he respected them i recited to the point of desperation i
walked
on my toes around the girls i shouted at the watchman:
"sure it's
easy for you because i am a poor defenseless white"; and
it occurred to me to insult him on a cultural matter
to; offend the girls too by this opportunity although they

were beginning to like me
"sure" i said "it's easy for you because i'm the last white'

i offended all 40 PhD curators honoris
causa; of museums electrical engineers astrologers spe;
cialists in space sci; ences atlantologists col; lectors of pre
columbian objects brigadier generals oceanographers his;
torians
cartographers spe; cialists in psychological warfare
researchers of pa
rapsychology libraries of congress and of universities
cultural bureaus archives bookstores instructors ex-pilots so
cieties for the investigation of the unexplainable mathe-
maticians
mythologists philologists retired colonels and other who
parti
cipated by suggestions decrees and corrections to my present
state they were offended from a cultural POV
as well as the girls who felt; offended from a national-sexual
POV
but protested weakly because they were beginning to like
me and;
they didn't want to interrupt me even though their calves
reddened with
indignation while; i recited by myself i shouted Isis was sta
nding beside me she said nothing anymore

(then i knew that the time had come for me to leave
the corridor and go
toward the swamps.)

IV

■ □ ■ □ ■

THE LADDER

1. NOW, AS I WRITE, RAIN WASHES ACROSS MY WINDOWS. I feel cold even though I'm sheltered, coiled up like a sad old monkey, here in my room with these sheets of paper before me.

Perhaps to avert the damp reverie haunting me, the face of a senile man comes to mind. I talked to him a few days ago during a break from my reading in a library. He was working on a book about the great terrors that are usually forgotten by historical memory . . .

"Any library is a minefield," he said, "because it contains the entire blessed and vile thinking of human beings. And if an idea lost in who-knows-what pamphlet ignored by everyone met its detonator, which lies in another, equally ignored pamphlet, the explosion would shake the whole universe . . ."

He bored me. I could see him trembling between the bookshelves . . .

Then the echo of a ride buried in one of my old texts entreats me: at night, on a bus, in the empty streets of the city. The driver had fallen asleep at the wheel and was driving with his eyes closed. On the bus there was, besides me, only one passenger, an albino who was holding a book, I *smelled* it, I could guess by the smell its title and the name of the writer: Huysmans, to whom I didn't do justice back then . . .

Naturally, the sheets of paper on which I write, and which I destroy or save, emanate auras, well-defined effluvia, and much more, just as do object-books or people. I recall that I recently encountered this observation in the book on the life and teachings of the Great Jetsun Milarepa, whom, unfortunately, I've ignored for so long. I refer to the words addressed to him by the Incomparable Marpa the Translator, when the young Jetsun, still a novice even though a great wizard, wanted to put his books, which he carried in a bundle, next to the books of the Master, as a reverential gift.

"Get your old papers out of here!" the Translator shouted. "They've started to contaminate my sacred relics and books and they'll give them a cold . . ."

I look at the blackened sheets of paper in front of me with an acute sense of the ridiculous. However, I stubbornly try to find meanings in them, the more logical, the flimsier. A hint of a beginning of a hierarchical system urges me to distinguish the so-called important meanings from the others, even to separate them by conscious criteria, but, naturally, I give up.

"I think, therefore I am not," I say to myself and laugh in earnest. I would laugh at any other similar stupidity. For instance, if I thought myself to be the shadow of an alien thought realized outside any phenomenal existence but up to its ears in the tradition of mental conflicts . . . Am I the thinker or the thought? Or: who is thinking me? And so on . . .

Then I decide to resume the tiring evocation exercise and go back to the distant time of the second corridor . . .

*Nim, a two-and-a-half-year-old chimpanzee, studies six hours per day with three young women at Columbia University. So far he has managed to learn 55 signs that he correctly uses to ask for various things.

2. Soon after Dragoş's departure we moved out of Maria's studio. Since she hadn't stopped by for quite a while, we left a note on the table with the requisite thanks for her hospi-

tality and our new address. We put the key in the usual spot, a hollow in the wall above the door.

We lived now on Română Square, above a high-rise. I say "above" because, by a hard-to-comprehend caprice of the architect, on the roof of the high-rise a few rooms had been erected in a row on one side, some sort of aerial cages connected by a narrow corridor and isolated from the rest of the building, as if they had fallen from the sky.

In those cages, apparently abandoned by their owners, nobody lived. Among the cages was a toilet whose window opened onto the black dampness of a so-called light well. Next to the toilet was an uninhabited little room, and then a blue curtain riddled by time tried to cover the empty space of the communal shower that was used, fortunately, only by us.

At the far end of the corridor a French window left a clear path for the light. Beyond it stretched the vast, dusty, and deserted roof-terrace. You could get there either directly, through the aforementioned French window, or by the fire escape, a ladder that began at the corridor below us where washrooms, drying rooms, and some of the utility rooms were lined up; the ladder was otherwise useless, because I never saw a living soul climb toward the hot tar of the roof. I myself ventured only once as far as its edge, which was surrounded by eaves of thin tin. From up there I could see how that anthill of people tiny as fingernails moved about in the street below and I became dizzy . . .

Our little room was six feet long and six feet wide. Zenobia had found it. It was furnished too: a sofa that had retired long ago and a chair that was still good. Nothing else would fit. We completed the furnishings by buying a big pillow and a length of white linen for bedsheets. We hammered a few nails in the walls for my two spare shirts and the two dresses acquired through Zenobia's honest labor. The books (we possessed a certain number of them), together with the other personal goods (our shared plate, two spoons, a mug with a color picture in which a little girl in national costume received her portion of gingerbread from a rural old man), were deposited by us partly on the chair, next to my papers, and partly under the sofa.

*Refusing food and water, Sandra, a female elephant in the Circo do Brasil, passed away. Twenty-four-year-old Sandra couldn't bear the separation from Helmut Chome, her young trainer, who had married and gone on his honeymoon.

3. A week later I ran into Maria. She was with Ioachim, they were talking in the street, wait a second while I light my cigarette.

I had known this Ioachim (an academically perfected cog) for a long time, both through Maria and from the street. We usually exchanged a few words in passing. He was a few years my senior, but that didn't matter. He wrote reviews and manipulated concepts. If he seemed a little more flexible than the others, it was only to the extent of appearing more open than his masters, and it was fitting that he took their place.

Otherwise, he was short, thin, well-proportioned, and too cute. He also seemed cultivated, he even knew one of my lines by heart, he recited it to me in greeting every time we met. I wanted to respond by kicking him in the pants but I restrained myself.

Maria couldn't stand him, that's what she said. The year before, he proposed to her, but she refused. (He was a colleague of her mother's in the same university department and that might have been reason enough.) "He's a cretin," she explained to me at the time.

I for one wasn't interested in what Ioachim said or wrote. That was his business . . . I knew a few others like him, some were even brilliant, their minds ran smoothly. A bunch of robots voluntarily frozen in their professional mechanism. They analyzed the tomb of pohetry, the wreath and the bouquets, but they avoided seeing the decomposed maiden inside or they saw her jumping about like a dead gymnast.

Besides, I tried to avoid Ioachim because every time I met him he triggered a strange physical sensation in me: it seemed that he dragged after him, through this world that is already smelly enough, a hard-to-bear mental stench.

Now he stood somehow aside, he didn't say a word. Maria clutched at me like a drowning person clutches at a straw.

"I'm glad I ran into you," she said. "I lost your address . . ." (She had misplaced it a few days ago, she didn't know how.)

I repeated the address to her, I explained how to get to our place, which floor, which stairs to take. We talked as if we were alone, Ioachim seemed not to hear us, he smiled and his eyes shone beautifully.

Once boys have completely entered the big lie of maturity, they are not exactly silent in these situations. As soon as they have an attractive young lady around, they rush in. A kind of blind frenzy pushes them to the fore, to cover the entire sonic space, leaving no room for the others. For some people this lasts until autumn, when their leaves fall, or even later. In the past, when the Inciter appeared, I too would unleash my eloquence. And even when I felt awkward, even when I made myself sick, I still found an excuse . . . That's why, perhaps, Ioachim started his motor. He spoke beautifully, his voice was warm and melodious . . .

In the beginning he expressed his admiration for our natural friendship (between artists) and I don't know what else. I felt like hitting him but I pitied Maria, she looked devastated, she glanced first at me, then at him, she seemed to implore me, she feared not to . . .

Ioachim went on talking. He said that my last pohem (where the hell had he read it?) was less disordering. (The expression is his.)

There was a tree near us in the street. The tree was feeding itself too, something like sap flowed through it, no, wait, a quiet unsettling flowed, downward or upward, it flowed unseen as oftentimes the mother of disorder flows through order, and the other way around, from beyond forms . . .

Ioachim tried to manufacture a metaphor, something about the pohetic chlorophyll, if you will, we studied this in botany class, besides he lived on the tree's dejecta in the middle of dejecta from a nature he didn't understand very well.

I finally took off. That Ioachim really smelled awful . . .

*The town of Maralal in Kenya was invaded by bees. The raging swarms fiercely attacked people and animals. Several people were taken to the hospital. Ultimately, the bees were neutralized thanks to the intervention of firefighters.

4. Perhaps I speak too seldom and too little of Zenobia. But I'll say that in those days she continued to weave around me a protective aura while I, stuck in the mud of passages, had started not to hear her whispers and not to see all her gestures that, surely, would have carried me to the water's edge.

Enveloped in the vainglorious axiom of our love, I felt her so attached, so incorporated in me that I almost didn't see her anymore, just as you don't see your own retina. In this way our deep, fanatical union melted into a double solitude whose only echo I concealed within myself like a talisman.

Sometimes I doubted even her exemplary existence: night after night she came home silent and exhausted. She persisted in an activity that I considered insignificant and unacceptable. If, at first, her hard labors in a sordid novelty shop where she cut and pasted letters and flowers on rags and pieces of cardboard seemed meant to cover too brilliant a life, now I saw in them a sort of resignation.

As I strove, as always, more toward a limitless possible than toward an ideal, I had the humiliating sensation that all her torture would amount to nothing but a demonstration of the pitiful truth that everything has its price.

Of course, it wouldn't have been too hard to make the simple gesture that would have solved at least our modest daily demands. But we avoided everything that seemed to be outside our love.

Every time I was distressed to see her extremely tired, she would say: "Don't worry, what you do is infinitely harder. When I can't do this anymore, I'll tell you . . ."

*The Colombian provinces of Cordoba and Sucre were deprived of electricity for more than ten hours because of swallows that provoked a short circuit by flying off from high-voltage power lines. Numerous enterprises, including bakeries, had their operations disrupted. As a result, at Sincelejo, the capital of Sucre, the population was deprived of bread for a day.

5. The sky was clear, not a leaf stirred. People went back and forth, all of them looked alive, even the dead, they gave me friendly smiles.

I had wandered a long time through the streets. It was late when I arrived, hungry and tired, in the center of the city. The asphalt was hot, I found a metal pencil without lead, the conscious temptation of experimenting made me anxious. It was about five in the afternoon.

Near the pool at the Lido a general relaxation, a kind of harmless benevolence floated in the air. I asked the doorman for permission to peek inside, he said it was possible, even though I was rather shabby-looking. He was a generous person . . .

The water of the pool made blue waves, beautiful women were swimming, bronze boys were making broad gestures, their words gathered in an enveloping hum, others were sitting at white tables on white chairs, they had tall glasses filled with sparkling ice cubes in front of them, "It's great," I said to myself, I could have sworn that I was cooling off in the water of the pool.

After a while, the doorman said: "Go on, beat it, I've let you see enough." I thanked him: "It's beautiful at your place, I'll come again." I beat it. "How gentle these people are!" I said to myself. "They all have their pockets crammed with candy, if I asked one of them where such-and-such street is, he'd surely answer me, and he'd also treat me to a piece of candy . . ."

I stopped in front of the windows of a café, the water in the café was blue as well, but the people bathing in it sat on couches and comfortable chairs upholstered in scarlet plush, the glasses and spoons shone, I was looking in the windows, the beautiful swimmers were not there but, instead, at a table close to the window sat an elderly man wearing an impeccable frock coat, his white hair and beard shone, the gentleman leaned on a cane with a silver knob, he was very distinguished, a little boy in a white suit with a lace collar sat on the chair next to him, they consumed something with whipped cream . . .

"These are my kind of people!" I said to myself, and I smiled to them through the window, I blew them kisses, I saluted them with my hand to the cap, I shouted "Kisses!" they looked puzzled, they gazed in wonder, they didn't know me, how could they?

I was looking at that old man and thinking: "What a difference between his frock coat and Dragoş's rough shirt . . ." But maybe Dragoş didn't even exist, Maria could never see him, neither could Jason, and I believe that little Empedocles wasn't seen by anyone but me. Maybe even the gentleman at the table didn't exist. That was his business . . .

Then I felt a cold void inside, like wet plaster. I sat down on the curb near the window. I don't know how long I stayed there, but after a while the gentleman came out pulling the little boy by the hand, they stopped in front of me.

"You wanted to tell me something, young man?" he asked.

"No, no," I answered. "I didn't want anything . . ."

The distinguished gentleman shook his head, he threw a coin to me, as you throw coins in the crossroads after the dead, behind the hearse, and he left.

I picked up the coin and threw it furiously after him.

Then I got sleepy even though it was still early.

"Go to sleep, you cretin," I said to myself and slowly set off toward home.

*The French librarian Louis Périn, while making an inventory of the objects used by readers as bookmarks and forgotten between the pages of the volumes at the library where he works, noted— besides postcards, greeting cards, and letters—ties, shoelaces, combs, toothpicks, parsley leaves, cheese rinds, fish bones, strips of bacon, and an unexecuted will.

6. On the boulevard there were too many noises, cars, carriages, streetcars, agitated people . . . I turned off into quiet side streets. After the serene wandering in the daytime, I was tempted by requital: a strange lucidity made me feel the soft floating of the earth with all that was on it. I feared that I would become detached, that I would fall up or down (it was the same thing). I tried to keep as close as possible to trees, lampposts, metal fences, or anything else that I could grab if need be.

Fortunately, this state didn't last long, it had passed by the time I reached Ioanid Park. I sat there on a bench, I wanted to pick a flower for Zenobia, there were enough of them, too bad it wasn't completely dark yet: in the dark, by the light of my hands, I could have chosen better.

A tranquil stillness had settled in the air. I think that I stood up from the bench and stepped over the lawn toward the flower beds. Then the earth covered me with a solid crust, the grass and the flowers invaded me, they grew out of me.

It's rather difficult for me to describe that state of vegetalization. I'll only say that I had been in it several times. Once, in an incident with a white fish, I lay stretched out on a divan in a large room, a vestibule, I couldn't move a finger. I felt awfully good inside, I felt, as in the park, a boundless reconciliation. I loved in a perpetual and amazingly simple present everything that existed, tears ran down my cheeks, I couldn't stop them, I didn't even want to . . .

I was paralyzed by the happiness of a kind of overwhelming and unmotivated regret. I reviewed and simultaneously unfolded my whole life. It was as if, working with several equations, the common unknown had shed its circumstantial crust and, renouncing itself, had turned into something whole and total, and the numbers, each one of them terribly alive, had found again their dimensionless character, and so on . . .

That's how one dies, I know this, drowned in an intense and tender melancholy, and for me, being born under a solar sign, melancholy is related to moisture.

I simplify a lot, but anyway . . . Maybe sometime I'll mumble more things about death and everyone will say "I knew that" and forget . . .

Until then, the dead are dead, with their time and movement. Corpses are something else, and my apparent toughness will never be able to bear a corpse up close. I saw a lot of dead people, I got along pretty well with them. But only two corpses: the first time was near Brebu Monastery when I stumbled on a funeral procession; in front walked a man who carried in his arms a cardboard box with no lid, with a doll inside as big as a two- or three-year-old child; at first I thought I was attending a procession for rain or something similar, and only after the people had passed did I realize that in the cardboard box I had unwittingly seen the corpse of a child . . .

(I'll say also that a few moments ago, while I was finishing the above sentence and was wondering why I wrote about corpses, I was interrupted by Mica, the woman who brings the milk every morning, who informed me that the little girl who drowned this winter and disappeared beneath the ice on the river was found today, May 5, caught in the branches of the tree submerged in front of the place called "The Wreckage." That's why I won't continue with the second corpse, of which I saw only the foot, yellow as a lemon, protruding from behind a screen in a hospital morgue, where I had accidentally ended up.)

I sat again on that bench in Ioanid Park. I struggled to extract one thing from another, and it wasn't at all easy. I couldn't tell for sure whether I had gone over the lawn toward the flower bed, even though I held in my hand the flower I had picked for Zenobia, I could have eaten it, I wasn't hungry, I kept it.

*The Physicians Council of Chile is examining a strange burn that a strong beam of light of unknown origin made on a 12-year-old child. The wound on the child's right shoulder has perfect geometric forms—two concentric circles and several dots of identical size. The child's mother maintains that the burn keeps changing color, turning in succession from red to brown and then to yellow.

7. Perhaps it would be fitting to say here that I had always felt around me the all-encompassing presence of a feminine principle that, when I tried to define its features, to give it a face, I named the Woman Spirit. But my receptiveness, still immature, succeeded only in creating the image of a giant woman, as big as the world.

Mother of mothers, ferocious and indifferent, gentle and generous, deaf, primitive, and infinitely superior to my rude masculinity, she protected me, she shielded me, she guided me through the complicated appearance that envelops us like the air we breathe, without being aware of it. The brutality of the image and the tragic character of the dimensions obscured the brightness of the intuitive concept, they amputated its promises, they took it into the zone of the anomalous and grotesque, where only promiscuity would have felt at home.

Besides, certain facts made me discover in myself reactions that were unequal in a suspect way. Once I ran away from a circus performance when a troupe of dwarf Polish ballerinas wearing loud makeup and dressed in transparent little dresses entered the arena. (On the other hand, the bearded lady seemed like a good joke to me: I had a photo of one from Denmark, I kept it with my pohems, I would have been sorry to find out that she had shaved off her beard.) In regard to the very few girls whose height was way above normal, I positioned myself between humor and pity. So, when I was about sixteen it so happened that Mother was visited by the daughter of a friend from the provinces whom I didn't know. Mother came into my room (I was doing my homework) and asked me to keep her guest company for a little while, until she finished something in the kitchen.

"She's very pretty," she said.

I went to keep her company. She was a blue-eyed girl about my age. She smiled timidly. She was more than six feet tall . . .

I was looking at her. At first I wanted her to carry me in her arms, to rock me, to walk me in the parks, with her giant-child face.

Then I got mad: it was difficult to bear the regression that she unwittingly forced upon me, throwing me back into a physical childhood that I had just escaped.

"Wait a minute," I said. "I'm going out to get a ladder to climb up and kiss you . . ."

I went into the yard. I came back with the ladder. I laughed like a brute. The giant girl was crying, she had bent over a little and was crying.

I leaned the ladder against a wall and fled . . .

*In 1895, California miners found the remains of a woman 80 inches tall. Three years later, a group of anthropologists discovered another female skeleton 94 inches tall. Similar skeletons were found in 1874 in North Carolina and in 1912 in Wisconsin. In 1930, the tombs of an ancient people who were 96 inches tall were discovered in northern Mexico.

8. Shortly before I left for the swamps, the concept and the physical attributes of the Woman Spirit had balanced again. I mean to say that, for instance, the prefigured giantism had become for me a kind of purely spiritual, abstract, fluid, and formless dimension, in which immensity and smallness, anomaly and naturalness, promiscuity and splendor coexisted, without existing as such.

I had started to intuit the total active indifference included in its most direct solicitations: imagine a lighthouse on the seashore at night during a storm; while the mad Keeper sends signals to *all* ships, *each individual* ship struggles unnoticed and alone in the dark. The flash of light doesn't render the cliffs visible anymore . . .

A vague causal link, however, made me believe in the beneficial effects of a certain behavior on which I won't insist so that I leave to each one the pleasure of finding it again, between mortification and debauchery.

(Zenobia calls this: to behave.)

9. I lay stretched out on the sofa thinking of the Woman Spirit. The feeling of vegetalization, that timeless second when she had caressed me like a serene, distant wing of death, still persisted in me.

Naturally, this wasn't our first encounter. But each time the premonition of death, whose direct logic didn't bother me at all, triggered only as an effect of another evocation, whereas now . . .

This time, in the park, I had evoked Zenobia (for me they had become almost twin sisters, in a way). I wondered, without separating them, which of the two brought me the news of gentle and distant death?

But let's drop it . . . My pohetic habits refuse to obey any order but their own, where clarity is an underground quality, equally necessary to the one that receives too . . .

That's why I started to think of another annunciation.

This occurred at a chalet in the mountains in northern

Moldova, shortly before I left for the swamps. Outside, the clouds jumbled together and dissolved in no time to make way for a sun that was so bright it looked wet.

I was alone in the largest room of the chalet, I sat on the bottom step of the stairs that led to the second-floor bedrooms. I don't know why, but that giant girl whom I had offended a long time ago came to mind. I was ashamed of myself, I should have stretched out my hand and stroked her hair a little, she was cute, I haven't seen her since. I had behaved like a spoiled brat, and so on, memories and regrets. My heart darkened . . .

After a while, I turned around slowly and looked at the stairs behind me. On the highest step another female giant stood motionless. I recognized her immediately, I even knew her name. She was a famous athlete, I had seen her in the newspapers and at the movies, in the newsreels.

She had stopped and looked down, over me. She seemed not to see me. I had the sensation that I was on Olympus, that gods were descending. That's how Cybele or the armed Athena or Artemis returning from the hunt must have appeared to the chosen ones. Her height seemed natural to me now, it didn't make me nervous.

Then the Woman Spirit climbed down, stepped around me without noticing me, and left the chalet. Outside, she took off her sandals. She sat on two chaise longues in the sun. She stretched her legs out on one of them, folded out with an extension.

Someone in a room upstairs turned on the radio. She lay on the chaise longues and listened. She tried to follow the rhythm with the tips of the toes of her bare feet.

I had gone outside after her. I stood respectfully aside, as was fitting, and I measured the difference between the rhythm that she kept and the one that I kept. To cover the distance from the ear to the tip of her toes the rhythm needed a fraction of a second more. In my case the rhythm became movement as soon as it reached my ear.

We stayed there until the sky clouded over again. It was rather chilly. The Woman Spirit got up from the chaise longues, put her sandals on, and went back inside the chalet. I left, the wind was blowing.

I traversed a kind of desert covered by rough and restless weeds, they spoke of rain, then a cold drizzle started, my skin felt like a wet shirt, I wanted to find shelter somewhere, I found myself in a valley, in front of a freshly whitewashed little house, I knocked at the door, an old woman opened it.

"Come in," she said, and I went in, a thread of fire burned in the room, but it was still cold and rather dark, anyway it wasn't raining inside, and I couldn't have found another shelter close by, the old woman gave me a little three-legged stool, then she spoke to someone, to a body that lay dissolved by the foggy light in the bed next to the wall: "Get up," she said, "'cause someone's here."

The person in the bed tried to get up (later, when I met Dragoş, I realized how much he resembled him, they both had the same long hair, the same yellowish-white beard, except the clothes of the person in bed were new and clean, he looked like he was dressed to go out . . .)

"No, please," I said. "I don't want to disturb you."

He put his head back on the pillow, he lay there quietly, I had gotten used to the semidarkness in the room. I had even begun to make out the old man's eyes covered by a thin bluish membrane, the Woman Spirit wanted to give me something to eat, I declined, "Take an egg at least," she said, I took a hard-boiled egg, I didn't eat it, I put it in my pocket.

"Is he ill?" I asked, nodding toward the man in bed.

"No, thank God," she said, "but we're waiting for him to die. I'll go live with my daughters 'cause they're all married in another village, he don't want to go with me, he says he's lived long enough, I'll stay here for a while so he won't die alone . . ."

I pulled the little chair next to the bed and waited there for about an hour until my clothes dried, the old man didn't say a word, I could see him well, he lay on his back with his eyes wide open, serene and quiet, like someone who had finished his business.

After a while I realized that in his apparent immobility he made, however, a rather strange gesture: he kept his right fist against his right knee and with one finger, the index finger, he stealthily drew a continuous circle over the rough wool of his trousers.

(I add that I had seen this sign once before, at the house of an old poet who lay on a swing, I would have taken him in my arms to rock him like a baby but next to me was the woman who, in the distant past, was his lover and muse. She had just came back from a funeral, she told us about things there, the poet balanced sadly in his serenity, he was silent and he turned his right index finger in a circle on his right knee, he closed a circle, a few days later he died . . .)

10. Late in the day, when Zenobia came back, I passed beyond quietness. I had been seized by a terrible apathy, I felt that I was falling, without shoulders or wings, in a void without sounds or landscapes. I lived in a state of nonexistence, a collapse into the void, from which I didn't want to escape.

There was a desert inside me, a desert without end; the wind whistled, the sun of the Sahara burned inside me, I was covered by sand. It was ugly and bad inside me, I would have preferred to die a thousand times rather than feel that desert anymore.

Usually, for me such states anticipated or completed the attainment of points that were too high and hard to bear. (Just think of it: I had wandered alone where others are carefully guided . . .) I knew the mechanism of their elimination, but every time, as chance would have it, I forgot it. This failure of my memory seemed to be the sign, the fundamental condition of requital . . .

Zenobia had turned on the lights. I stared, without seeing, at the ceiling. It wasn't I who wanted to die but my flesh, my bones, I don't know how to phrase this. Actually, even they didn't want anything; they were only following the law, as if it were a final link. And it wasn't a matter of death, because death, the same as life, is beyond this law.

"What's the matter?" asked Zenobia, and her worried voice brought me back to the surface in a second.

"The matter is that I *can't* anymore and I don't *want* anymore," I said.

"What happened to you?" (She gently caressed my forehead.) "What have you done?"

I told her in detail, but the events of the day, now lacking the sap of life and reduced to words, seemed banal and insignificant. I had wandered the streets, I had met Maria and Ioachim, I had found a metal pencil and I don't know what else, I had consciously wished for something different, I had stopped in front of a pool, I had rested in a park, I had picked a flower for her ("It's over there on the chair"), I had thought of some old encounters, and what of it? These kinds of things can happen to anyone and no one pays any attention to them. Why am I systematizing them? Why am I building traps for myself? Why am I torturing myself so much? (Actually, I knew, but I waited for her to tell me.)

"You shouldn't have thrown that coin away," said Zenobia, and I knew that in the course of my movements that was when I had made a mistake.

"It's all right, I'll go get it tomorrow. I'll find it for sure . . ."

Actually, it didn't matter at all whether I found it or not. I felt like laughing, but I sighed: "See how I brag?"

"You lack self-confidence again," said Zenobia. (Now she was smiling.)

*At the Zoological Institute of the University of Saarbrücken, a swarm of bees flying in an area with high-voltage power lines was seized by panic, attacking each other and killing their queen. Then they sought refuge in their hives, where they proceeded to a kind of collective suicide by plugging all the holes through which air could enter.

11. That night, perhaps because she had seen me sad, Zenobia remembered our games and she asked for pencil and paper. I handed them to her along with the piece of cardboard that served me as a table when I wanted to write. Then I turned off the lights in the room and in the corridor, and I crouched between the sofa and the wall in order not to disturb her.

Stretched out on the bedsheet in the dark, Zenobia started to draw.

After a while (I noted, as usual, the duration of the game: first drawing—half an hour, the second, a little longer), I realized that she had fallen asleep. Then, trying not to wake her, I gently lifted the pencil from her chest, I turned on the light and read the title of the first drawing, written calligraphically with particular proficiency although Zenobia hadn't used her hands and eyes to do it: "Zenobia in My Life."

Even without the title I would have recognized my features because the time such a game lasted represented for me the beginning of a state of indescribable serenity where I felt each and every hyphen, each and every letter, each and every digit with their meaning that came from beyond us, and because *after that* I managed to understand, with a lucidity that amazed me, the most cryptic signs. Here's the plain, straightforward description of the drawing:

In the center there was the outline of my face, without ears, like a strange and diaphanous mask. The eyes, smaller and farther apart than mine, seemed to look inside. The line of the chin looked like a caress of the pencil. The mouth, very much accentuated, dominated all three elements of the face. (I had between my teeth my old pipe *en corne*.) And the eyebrows emphasized an essential space above which my forehead and hair melted together in wreaths of smoke.

Pressed against my cheek, where my left ear should have

been, was Zenobia. She appeared like a giant earring or an infusorian lamp reaching down to the end of my chin. She was portrayed like a circle with thirteen cilia, of which three were doubled, all on the left side. The third, fourth, and seventh cilia began under the superior median line.

In the interior of the first circle was outlined a second one formed by numerous eyebrows that surrounded the inner eye. The first circle (the one at the exterior), accentuated here and there by two or even three lines, rested on two little legs, the space between them shaded, encrusted in an apparent oval support that inclined to the left. To the right of the oval, a line between Zenobia and me, also inclined to the left, touched the lower part of my chin. Vertically, Zenobia didn't surpass the apples of my prominent cheeks; downward, with her little legs and all, she barely reached the end of my chin.

To the right of the drawing a thin, sharp cone of shadow, pointing upward, marked the void.

The sensation of diaphanous strangeness was particularly conveyed by the ensemble, seemingly created from transparencies and pallors . . .

I won't describe the second drawing, entitled "The State of the World." I'll say only that it began in the lower part with a multitude of cripples who squirmed in the large box of the malady of the conscious and ended at the top of the pyramid, under a star, where there was no one left . . .

*The young Belgian, Chantal Sabine Derycke, lived for ten months behind a wall built in a garage in the village of Corinaldo, near Ancona. The carabinieri discovered her by accident, almost starved and lying in the stench of the enclosure where she had been put by her lover, the carpenter Marcello Montesi. The enclosure had only one little window near the roof and was well concealed from the outside. Through that little window Montesi would occasionally throw his prisoner something to eat.

12. Two days later I found a note attached to the door of our room. In it Maria asked me to come see her without fail in

regard to a very important matter. She would wait for me on the afternoon of the next day at her place, not at the studio (she had underlined the words *without fail* and *my place*). "My folks are out of town until Monday, so you'll be spared the pleasure of meeting them again this time," Maria ended her message.

The next day was Saturday, we could have gone to the movies, but Zenobia insisted that I answer her appeal, she said that I was selfish, that I didn't care about others, who might need me, and so on. Finally, she persuaded me, and I set off in the late afternoon for Maria's place.

I walked slowly, some rather ugly clouds scudded across the compact and glassy sky. The city lay in its carpet of dust. I felt outside any favorable link with those clouds gathered under my eyes in a jumble seemingly meant to demonstrate to me how illusory our receptiveness could sometimes be . . .

I continued, however, to walk silently and cautiously through the people who rushed to their burrows. Streetcars stood still on their tracks, there was no electricity. Above us the Storm-being lay in wait, ready to pounce . . .

*In Walnut Creek a large number of migratory birds dart at cars and at house windows. Experts think that the birds get intoxicated by consuming wild fruit that contains toxins whose effects resemble those of alcohol.

13. Maria had been waiting for me, who knows how long, she opened the door before I could knock. The wind blew in as I entered.

"I was afraid you wouldn't come," she said; she seemed frightened.

I passed through two or three rooms on the way up to her room, I won't describe it. I'll only say that there were, among other things, two armchairs, a little table, and a sofa. I might have liked her room had I not seen in the crepuscular light a six- or seven-year-old girl squirming on the carpet.

Even so small, the girl reminded me in a strange way of that lonely girl that I had seen toward spring in the middle of the swamps . . .

"It's my sister," said Maria. "She has a stomach problem, she's having an attack."

From outside, from the garden, you could hear the branches of the trees cracking. The Storm-being pressed against the sashes as if avoiding the fragile glass; it tried to break everything with a single blow.

"The windows!" screamed the little girl. "They could break . . . !"

I went to the window, I was thinking that neither Maria nor her sister had ever slept in the forest, that they had never heard thousands of branches rumbling at once, and that's why . . .

I was holding the windowpane with the palms of my hands, it was a beautiful piece of glass, curved slightly outward, with mother-of-pearl iridescence. The carpentry looked solid, the window could withstand the pressure. The little girl moaned, she wanted to throw up, Maria held her head, she didn't know what to do.

This lasted for a while, I couldn't say how long, the little girl calmed down a little; "I'm going to put her to bed," said Maria, she helped her stand up and they both left. You could hardly see in the room. I sat in an armchair and I waited for about a quarter of an hour until Maria came back.

"I put her to bed," she said. "She was afraid . . ."

She went toward the switch, she wanted to turn on the lights.

"It doesn't work," I said. "There's no electricity . . ."

She tried. The lights didn't work (when such things happen people forget them immediately, as if that could solve anything . . .).

Maria sat, in the dark, in the other armchair, it seemed to me that she held her hand over her mouth, I could hardly make out her features.

"The two of us," I said, "haven't talked in a long time. In the meantime, for your information, we've gotten bored with the city, Zenobia and I. Maybe we'll go back to the swamps . . ."

I talked for the sake of talking. I listened to myself and that's all.

Maria didn't say a word. I fell silent too.

I sat quietly in the armchair, I looked in her direction, we were alone in the room yet I felt another presence, I suspected that it was supposed to be this way, I waited for her to tell me what she had to say.

"Do you mind if I lie down on the sofa?" Maria asked after a while. "It would be much easier for me . . ."

"Do as you please," I answered.

She lay on the sofa, I saw her as some indefinite form.

Then, unexpectedly, that form mumbled: "What do you have against me? Why are you against me . . . ?"

Perhaps it was Maria who had spoken, but the thick brutal voice wasn't hers.

14. Everything had became idiotic and comical but I didn't feel like laughing. I pitied Maria, the form stretched on the sofa could have been hers or someone else's, but the voice, in any event, was Jason's.

"Why don't you answer me?" it asked.

"You're crazy," I said. "What could I have against you? I had almost forgotten that you existed . . ."

A sparrow struck the windowpane, it wanted to get in. It fell there, outside . . .

"You're wasting your time trying to trick me . . . !" Jason (or maybe Maria) shouted. "You can't forget that back then I kicked both of you, you and that Zenobia of yours . . ."

"Leave her out of this." (He had begun to bore me.) "You'd better tell me why you wanted to see me, and let's get it over with . . ."

Jason (or maybe Maria) fell silent for a while. I was wondering whether I should stay or go.

I felt that the state of danger had dispelled. The Stormbeing had left us. The world sank into silence. I heard a horseshoe strike the pavement, far away.

"Do you think that I don't know why you didn't kick me?" he began again. "You're tougher than me, you could've kicked back . . ."

"What are you babbling about?" I asked him (I don't know why Erigena and the others plus their opposites had come to mind. Each one, helped by the others, built traps for himself, and, helped by the others, fooled himself . . .).

"You wanted to humiliate me, that's why you didn't kick me, right?"

I felt gentle and aggressive at the same time. Actually, I use different words for a balanced state that language hesitates to grasp in its pliers. Perhaps I did the same in my mother's womb, or before, or after (I don't know after *what*). I undoubtedly intuited why Zenobia had insisted that I come here and I waited to reach the end of a meeting that, for me, had already ended.

"Why don't you answer me?" Jason had raised his voice again. "Do you think that only you know? There are still others in the world. For instance, I—"

"Jason," I said, "maybe that very knowledge of yours is to blame. You failed in your apprenticeship. You turn the lights on and off and that's not enough for you, you want more than you deserve . . ."

"You talk like a pope, but that's all right," he said. "Maybe you'll still help me . . ."

He seemed resigned. He asked me what he should do about a certain thing. I told him that, of course, I didn't know. Then we both fell silent, I remained in the armchair. There was good or evil in the world but neither good nor evil existed anymore . . .

Then Maria sighed, it was she who sighed this time . . .

*Nine young speleologists from Dijon, who had disappeared in the Glaz caverns, in the Alps, were found in a gallery 100 yards below the surface.

15. After a while, Maria woke up, she sat on the edge of the sofa. Perhaps she was a favorable person, I won't explain what I understand by this, I'll say only that it's about something that is outside love, with which it is almost always confused.

"It would be good to turn on the lights," I said. "I think the electricity is working now."

She stood up, went in the dark to the switch, and turned on the lights. She looked exhausted, bleary-eyed, she sat in the other armchair in front of me. She remained bent over, her forehead touching her knees. We were among visible things. The storm had left us completely.

We sat like this for I don't know how long, without saying a word. Then Maria lifted her face to me.

"I would like to ask you something," she said. She spoke with her own voice but in whispers, as if she feared being overheard by someone. "Promise me that Jason will never find out about your talk . . ."

"Jason doesn't know?" (When I uttered his name the lights didn't go off, they didn't even flicker.)

"He doesn't," answered Maria. "You talked to him, but he doesn't know. And if he finds out, he's capable of killing me . . ."

There was so much fear in her words that I hastened to assure her that Jason wouldn't find out anything, ever, from me. Then I casually asked her:

"Do you know what we talked about?"

"It's rather complicated," she answered. "I was sleeping and I had a nightmare with you two face to face. I still have it . . ."

"Try to forget it," I said. "Imagine it never happened . . ."

"I imagined so many things, maybe too many," sighed Maria. "I've had enough . . ."

She pressed her forehead against her knees again and remained that way. She seemed to be sleeping. She didn't even budge when I got up from the armchair, or when I left her room.

16. At home I told Zenobia, without omitting a single detail, the whole story of my meeting with Jason and Maria. At first she listened attentively, then she smiled.

"Of course," I mumbled (I felt offended), "it's easy for you, you weren't in Maria's nightmare . . ."

But I remembered that, at one point, I too was almost ready to burst out laughing; Maria's speaking with Jason's deep and coarse voice seemed even stranger and more grotesque to me too.

"You're smiling because you weren't there," I repeated, I wasn't angry anymore.

"It's not that." Zenobia pointed her finger at me. "Look how you've put your trousers on . . ."

I looked and I saw the most unexpected thing of that evening: even though I hadn't moved from Maria's armchair, even though I had come directly home without stopping on the way, even though I had dressed normally in the morning and I hadn't undressed during the day, my trousers were on backward, that is, the side with the buttoned-up fly was in the back.

I don't know to what extent all this could be of interest but that is exactly how it happened and I couldn't leave it out.

V

■ □ ■ □ ■

THE LAST MEETING OF DANTE AND BEATRICE ON A COFFEE CUP MADE IN SWEDEN

I. WE HAD GREATER CONFIDENCE IN THE ISOLATION OF OUR corridor. It compensated us somehow for the burning heat in our room: since it became cooler only at dawn, we could leave the door open all the time.

It so happened that one night, when, stretched out on my back, I looked into the dark and meditated on who knows what, I heard a kind of rhythmic whisper, a moan repeated at fixed intervals. The moan was regularly followed by a light scratching sound, as if caused by a fingernail.

Zenobia was sleeping. "Do you hear that?" I asked her (in my mind, because I didn't want to wake her).

"Petru . . ." she answered (she was talking in her sleep, I didn't persist, I let her sleep).

I waited and listened. The sorrowful cries and the annoyingly soft scratching sound seemed to come from somewhere in front of the second room down the corridor, which I knew was uninhabited. We were separated from that room only by a tiny closet and the bathroom.

I went out into the corridor. In front of that second room, a light bulb attached to the wall was on; tiny moths hovered around it. Petru was crouched in front of the light bulb, near the door, on an extremely small rug, a doormat to wipe your feet on, apparently brought by him. He inhaled and exhaled his lament and scratched the ocher panel of the door with his fingernail.

*Pedro Miguel da Silva, from a village north of Bahia, lived for 40 years chained to a tree stump in a cave. He was chained there when he was 21 by his brother-in-law because of an apparent hysterical fit. After the brother-in-law's death, his two sisters continued to bring him food every day and to clean him up twice a week.

2. I sat beside him on the cement, my back against the wall, and I stayed that way for a while without saying a word. Now I could distinguish his lamentations: "Nathalia," he cried, "open up, Nathalia . . . !" I saw how he stretched out his hand, like a peduncle, how he scratched, how he retreated into himself, peduncle and all, as if into a shell.

I too could have stayed there forever, lamenting and scratching. My back adhered perfectly to the wall, a little blue butterfly had alighted on the edge of my shadow, and I remembered how exhausted Zenobia was . . .

"You're wasting your time," I said to Petru. "She doesn't want to open the door for you."

He looked at me, he had fog in his eyes, I don't know whether he saw me, he looked surprised.

After a while he shook his head. "Oh, it's you," he whispered. Then he resumed his lament: "Nathalia! Open up, Nathalia . . . !"

"She doesn't want to open the door for you," I repeated.

Petru turned to me again. He had stretched out one hand, he scratched in the air. "You don't understand, Laurențiu," he said (I accepted with a certain displeasure the name that wasn't mine). "She doesn't open up because they've beaten her. They've shaved her head and she's embarrassed . . . They've locked her inside. She can't open the door . . ."

He had taken his mouth out of the shell and spoken through it, and maybe he was thinking, somewhere in his crouching.

"You're calling her too softly," I continued. "Maybe she doesn't hear you or she doesn't recognize your voice because you call out too softly. And how could she possibly hear that scratching? You should knock loudly, with your fist. I can knock for you, if you want . . ."

I tore my back away from the wall, the little butterfly flew off from the edge of my shadow, it looked like I was about to stand up and knock at the door, although that wasn't my intention.

"No, no . . ." Petru objected. He had come out of the shell, he sat on the mat with his legs under him like a snake charmer before his basket, he didn't step even a fraction of an inch beyond the edges of the mat. The yellowish light of the bulb shone in the fog of his eyes. "No, no . . . We could frighten her. You don't know how easily she gets frightened . . ."

I remembered I once saw a man caressing a pig, but I felt pity for Petru. I would have jumped like a grasshopper under the light bulb. I would have done anything to help him. He didn't say anything, he wasn't lamenting anymore, he stared into the void.

Then all of a sudden he shouted: "Why are you hitting me?"

"Who's hitting you?" I asked.

"What have I done to you, Laurenţiu?" He was crying now. He had covered his face with his hands. "Why are you beating me?"

"Shut the hell up," I said, "people are sleeping . . ."

I was afraid he would wake Zenobia (she was so tired!), but he abruptly fell silent, crouched again on the mat, and resumed his lament: "Nathalia! Open up, Nathalia . . ."

I looked toward our room. Zenobia was there on the threshold, she gestured to me: "Leave him alone," I left him alone, I went back to our room. I closed the door, it was very hot.

*Twelve 17th-century paintings belonging to a museum in Arles were damaged by one or more people who slipped past the visitors and, using a sharp, pointed object, carefully perforated the eyes of the portraits.

3. I didn't sleep that night. It was like when you forget something important and the memory of forgetting tortures you, or when a barely prefigured thing catches you in the meanness of its unfolding and leaves the taste of remorse in your mouth, not knowing what you are guilty of.

Where had I gone wrong? Not here with Petru, because, undoubtedly, I had gone wrong before, somewhere else . . .

For a while I was assailed, of course, by explanatory temptations, by analogical lures, a kind of chasing of one's own tail capable, at most, of replacing one word with three or four others, equally barren and useless, confronted with which the Moirai can feel, and for good reason, offended.

To calm myself down, I told myself that that's what usually happens to me: when there is an agitated being around me, I feel bad. How many times did I get off the streetcar, for instance, because I had felt such a being around me . . .

Then, stretched out on my back, my eyes open, I remembered a shiny green little frog: once, some time ago, in the swamps, at the water's edge, she had stopped near me and given me an annoying stare. I said to her in a harmless way: "Come on, go swim." She didn't budge, she wanted at all costs to stick the cold suckers of her eyes on me.

Then I picked up a little stick, a reed, to chase her away. I didn't intend to hit her, I said to her once more: "Come on, get out of here!" I only wanted to scare her. But with a precision that expressed exactly my real goodness at that moment (maybe I was, as I am now too, without realizing it, on the Pyramid of the Dog), I hit a nerve, the most fragile, because the little frog suddenly somersaulted backward and remained stock-still, as if dead.

She floated obliquely, half-submerged in the water. I

looked at her and felt like crying. I rediscovered that I was separated from myself, in spite of all the trials I'd undergone. As a carrier of only one part, whatever that might be, I felt how the zone of the double squirmed, a zone from which I had believed myself protected. Perhaps what I'm saying is not clear. Anyway, it was a suffering of my structure . . .

After a while, the little frog started to move again. Then I became a little calmer: at least she was alive . . . But she persisted in playing the Big Game to the end. She spun spasmodically like a demented propeller, struggling at random like ten lame people, like twenty epileptics . . .

I continued to lie in the dark with my eyes wide open. Zenobia was sleeping quietly next to me. Through the door I could hear Petru's now-muffled lamentations. I tried not to see the spasms of that little frog. Behind her agonizing game I felt how the beginning of requital was triggered, unclear and perfidious. I was gradually losing the customary force of denial, the possibility of opposing the inverse temptations. I was tempted more and more by the trap-idea of consciously and ignobly using my possibilities.

At such moments, the difficulty lies in knowing, forgetting that you know, whether it's a matter of weakness only or whether what you take for weakness represents the frontier, at first always bewildering, of another zone. I was still *on this side,* the requital offered me pity for Petru as a justification. I had the foggy sensation that I had gone wrong, that I had gone astray but, above all, I wanted to take a look, to see Nathalia's room. And I saw . . .

*The police discovered almost one ton of dinosaur bones in a container at the Antananarive Railroad Station.

4. I was helped by some routine techniques abandoned since my adolescence. They had been revealed to me by a cat. Back then, she would lie on my chest every night, sleeping there like a tiny sphinx. Sometimes I turned the light bulb at

the head of my bed on and off. There were fears and vanities in my play: I wanted to demonstrate to her my power of making light or darkness.

She would remain motionless. Her retina contracted and dilated in turn; but our electric wonder seemed not to interest her.

However, because she liked me, one night she taught me to see; that is, to regain the sense that some natural beings still possess intact, while we humans only rarely regain this sense and always perceive it either as a gift or an infirmity. That night, I wouldn't have moved my eyelids for fear of disturbing my too gracious sphinx . . .

I won't insist on a state that I had almost forgotten. I'll say only that on the first night of Petru's lamentations I remembered it to satisfy the petty necessity of looking from my bed into that so-called room of Nathalia's. And I saw.

It was a small room, a little bigger than ours, full of rags and old stuff thrown haphazardly in there: a few broken and dusty chests, a few legless chairs one on top of the other, a spring mattress leaning against the wall with its legs in the air, a broken swing, a metal vase covered with verdigris, and so on. Nobody lived there, nobody could have lived there.

*The Shanka Indian tribe, which had fought the Incas and then retreated into the Amazon jungle, reappeared in northeastern Peru after four centuries.

5. For several weeks Petru's visits, accompanied by his sad lamentations, continued night after night. They were the signal or rather the highlight of some causalities, which I could call, for lack of another, equally approximate word, aberrant.

The very next day things started to develop upside down. The usual simple appearances seemingly turned against me. Everything became misleading. It was as if a powerful and irresponsible force wanted to include my movements in its incoherence. Whatever I would have done (because it still depended, to a certain extent, on me too) seemed cunningly undermined by that force or nature.

I lived, as usual, among alarm signals, waiting for a more and more indefinite something. "Actually, nothing serious is happening," I would say to calm myself. But threatened and weak amid the aggressive unleashing of unsure laws, I increased my confusion by tormenting myself to elucidate their mechanisms. My usual active indifference deserted me in favor of an obsessive need to find coherent guidelines. My direct perceptions, which I had sufficient reason not to trust too much, also dug at the foundation of the only certainty till then unshaken: the fact that I didn't know anything and that I didn't have to believe, at least for the time being, that I could have understood something.

Sometimes I blamed the numbers that I felt gliding above me again not as quantitative abstractions but as harsh laws of an incommensurable and inconvertible world. Then I consciously tried to get out of their secret, immersing myself all the more in it. But I don't want to talk about numbers right now, although they are capable of anything . . .

Take it anyway you like, this crepuscular blabber that belongs more to states than to meditative activities. Anyway, it would be a grave error to think that it has an explanatory nature. All I do is describe, and so on . . .

*The young Joëlle Lefevre, put to sleep by the hypnotist Alain Zuili, will try to sleep for 129 hours in a bed in the middle of a department store in Avignon. As she sleeps, she will be fed with orange juice mixed with other nutrients.

6. A sensation of vague panic, like when you are at a funeral, insinuated its equivocal echoes into me. And Petru's high-pitched, plaintive, and trembling voice sounded like a sad flute among them.

At the same time as his arrival, an increasingly severe blockage developed. By expressing it rather crudely and by admitting a few exceptions, I could define it as a divorce between my consciousness and my factual existence. The conflict between these two planes compensated, however, so efficiently that each plane seemed capable of literally pulverizing any temptation to escape from their common game.

Mental routines, even those of refusal, stopped me cold. Once in a while I got, of course, the simple idea of reexamining them, of bringing them into agreement with the bewildering data of events. Then I succeeded, for a while, in rejecting the acceptance of forms but I felt instead the more and more present harshness of that nature or force, which aggravated perfidiously, as if it were alien to my states, my stagnation caused by the blockage.

The ambiguity of duration and the ephemeral, the uncertainties of moral perfection and vileness, the impact of the unknown with the more and more tempting false certainties, held me within their zones of interference, imposing upon me desires, explanations, and withered impulses.

Beyond the appearance of my movements, that force, which could be a force of nature, became more and more decisive.

Now, when I write, its evocation, falsified by the involuntary intervention of imagination and equally blurred by the data of memory, makes things appear different than back then, when they were in full development. Besides, I realize how difficult it would be to accept, for instance, the statement that one of the primary underground causes of that blockage had its source precisely in my sad and conjunctive need of explanations . . .

I found myself in the position of an exhausted swimmer who fights to rescue from the waves a brother on the point of drowning, while that brother struggles and unconsciously pulls the swimmer with him, toward death . . .

*Surgeons discovered 300 coins and a variety of 200 metallic objects in the stomach of a man who was in the habit of swallowing everything that he could find.

THE LAST MEETING OF DANTE AND BEATRICE

7. Maybe all I'm doing is uttering a string of errors, but I have to say that at such moments the monsters of the imagination, not always imaginary, start to swarm around you.

Indifferent or not, they try to muddle even more the uncertain antinomy between good and evil, outside which you occasionally succeed in positioning yourself. In this way, scattering to the winds your poor behavioral solutions, they reverse the immediate effects of any thought process. Then, in the chaotic absolute that envelops you, the executioner can appear, or even be, an angel, and the angel an executioner, while the superintimate part placed at the core of the core of your being awaits in an impotent sadness the end of the time of passage.

All these developments, unavoidably obscure, usually appear cloaked in the guise of a perfect banality that constitutes the very crust of their development. Barely noticeable, they maintain themselves at the limits of an ambiguity ready at any time to prove to you that it can't be just a matter of simple coincidence . . .

As far as I'm concerned, an obstinate poetic fanaticism (the big trap of my life) aggravated my blockage by ever widening the gap between myself and the few poets that I could have loved. Nobody should perceive it as disdain or denigration when I state that each of them seemed to me to lose something of what had to be found, finding instead rather more of what had to be lost. More and more isolated, I clearly saw how the drop of grace, forgotten in the process, became diluted and, most of the time, a pretext or subject for intelligent theoretical texts, the more brilliant, the more treacherous, while poetic thinking, diverted from its mute riverbed, exhausted itself in beating against sterile banks.

In my perspective, the ancient mental malady of general requital replaced the poetic miracle in the world. But let's skip it . . .

Maybe I say all this to explain why, during the brief period of time that I'm now referring to, I had become terribly allergic to writing, which deprived me of a strong liberating aid. The habits of writing, at other times stimulating, at least from an emotional point of view, seemed to me more useless and more unsatisfying than ever, I even discovered for them a leading role among the intimate causes of my state . . .

*One morning, 12-year-old Trisha Reay woke up sneezing: she sneezed continuously at the rate of three sneezes per minute for a period of 204 days.

8. In order not to write, I talked. I had a strange feeling listening to myself: it seemed to me that I heard the voice of a stranger dissolving in its own rumble, like the wind in the desert. Of course, I continued to search for independent sounds but I realized that I was listening to the echo of my own dissolution.

The only fulcrum, itself marked by the perfect exhaustion of meanings, consisted in the fact that, even then, any pohetic fact seemed to me more of an ethical nathure, and ethical nathure, and so on . . .

Otherwise, talking to myself didn't solve anything. The physical mechanism of writing, which I had accepted for such a long time, was too much in my blood. The control, at least of its rate of revolution, left its mark here too, like it or not.

However, I continued to soliloquize. I tried direct and harsh communication techniques, which I won't insist on. But even then, the same as now, the pohetic volutes undermined my force of total rejection of control, maybe the only one capable of breaking the impasses.

All of this, as well as other things, determined me to return to writing. And, in order not to fall prey to writing again, I devised only already demolished constructions . . .

*Hideaki Tomoyori, 46, of Japan, succeeded in memorizing mathematical figures out to 15,151 decimal places.

THE LAST MEETING OF DANTE AND BEATRICE

9. By my side, Zenobia led her life on the most direct point of common appearance. An obvious fragility veiled her wonderful strength to the point that I myself, of whom she was a part, sometimes forgot her reality, like someone who, blinded by the light of the moon, forgets the sun or doesn't look at it so as not to burn his eyes.

Her daily existence, retired and unassuming, passed unnoticed. Attentive to the faintest vibrations from outside, she responded to them only with the fibers of the unseen miracle that still lies dormant in each of us.

In a world of signs, she deciphered signs in everything. She bowed silently, with deep respect, before them. The unexplainable seemed to have an unexpected clarity for her, and her life, unimportant and banal to others, constituted an uninterrupted ritual.

Like the waters of a river changing, as determined by the banks, their shape and depth but never their course from spring to sea, Zenobia, always worried about the prefigured weirs, knocked them from her path or quietly took a detour, without dividing her being at all.

Naturally, with regard to her, I won't insist on too much. The dangerous game of evocation has its own limits and logic, and it seems necessary to me to attenuate its ferocious power of attraction, ready to swallow you like a hungry stomach . . .

*Rhett Stevens succeeded in making 192 smoke rings from only one puff on a cigarette.

10. I had long given up the practice of meetings provoked consciously and unilaterally. Actually, I believed, perhaps mistakenly, that their significance had been, back then, only to draw my attention to a more general receptiveness capable at certain moments of guiding and bringing closer to me foreign joys and despairs meant to momentarily respond to appeals and then to go their own ways.

However, on one of those days, which I'll call Friday, I found myself walking the streets again. I wanted to meet Cornelius Agrippa in regard to a little clay pot.

Back then I felt a certain liking for Agrippa, whose letters of a miserable pyrotechnist (I refer especially to his letters to Abbot Tritheim) fell into my hands much later, causing his halo, tarnished enough already, to dim: my rudimentary Latin added to his none-too-brilliant Latin some secret implicit meanings capable of triggering certain imaginative mechanisms. A similar criterion urged me, for instance, to prefer the subtexts of Meister Eckhart to the texts of Jakob Boehme or, on a different level, to enjoy reading Raymond Roussel, whereas Joyce made me throw up.

(I know that these necessary allusions could suggest a system of culthural references, but I'm trying to express something else.)

I had met Agrippa several times under different circumstances and in different locations (Călăraşi, Jibou, Câmpulung-Muscel, Bucharest), always under the appearance of the same scabby black dog with teary and extremely expressive eyes, and a terribly human grin on its face.

He too had easily recognized me every time, even when, for personal reasons, I wouldn't have wanted him to. At one of our meetings I took a picture of him, he had benevolently consented. I sent the photo to that young lady from the Department of Classical Philology at the University of Bucharest because she insisted on having my portrait. I signed it neither von Nettesheim nor Naum, as would have been natural, but Raphael, perhaps thinking of the causes of the young painter's premature death—otherwise, he didn't interest me at all.

Agrippa wasn't one of the old visitors to my first corridor. I only met him while wandering in the streets, and each time we communicated only by glances, I couldn't tell in what human or dog language, but it happened exactly like that and not otherwise.

*Hugo Zacchini, a.k.a. the Human Cannonball, passed away at the age of 77. He was the first man to be shot from a cannon.

11. I had walked a lot, I was tired. I hadn't seen Agrippa. I wanted to be with Zenobia, to blame her, to say that because of her and her alone . . .

Toward evening, I entered a secondhand bookstore, a crummy place, where I hadn't been ever since I'd found bugs in the spine of a book that I'd purchased there. "You haven't dropped by in a long time," said the owner. I didn't answer, I went straight to the bookshelf to the right, something drew me there like a magnet, I pulled from the shelf an old volume bound in peeling reddish leather: Cornelius Agrippa, *De Occulta Philosophia*—a first edition. I didn't have any money, I put the book back and left.

I wandered through the streets some more. Had I met Agrippa or not? I thought that, anyway, at least something had worked. I thought of the pitiful logic of coincidences, I thought of not thinking anymore . . .

It had gotten completely dark when I met Constantin on a corner of Batiştei Street. He stood there in front of a light bulb, he had a humble, doggy smile on his face. Maybe he was waiting for someone; anyway, he didn't seem too happy to see me.

I asked him whether it was true that he had died. He mumbled something while the lower part of his cheek, blue from the too frequent use of the razor and crossed by a brick-red scar, turned bluer.

"You don't have to answer," I added. "I don't particularly want to know . . ."

At that moment, Jason passed by on the other side of the street, he didn't see us.

"There he goes again," I said. "Hopefully the lights won't go off . . ."

"Who's 'he'?" asked Constantin.

"Jason," I replied.

When I uttered Jason's name the lights on Batiştei Street flickered intensely (no, it wasn't my imagination). Constantin was rather frightened, I patted him on the back, he calmed down.

Then, remembering my question, he said that he hadn't died, how could he be dead when he was there in flesh and blood, at the corner of Batiştei Street?

"Damn them," he said, "they never tire of making up lies about this and that . . ."

Then he asked me whether I had an uncle who had exactly the same name as he, with even the same initial between the first and last names. When I answered yes, he told me that, actually, that uncle of mine had died and was buried at the Resurrection cemetery next to his father, Constantin's, that is; that both of them, that uncle of mine and his father, had names identical to his, Constantin's, so that at the Resurrection cemetery there were now two crosses on two tombs almost touching one another where lay two people who had nothing in common while alive, they hadn't even known each other, and only death, no one knows why, placed their identical names side by side, even the initial was the same . . .

"I think that this is the cause," he said. "Someone must have read the obituary in the newspaper about your uncle's death, or must have walked through the cemetery and seen the name on the two crosses side by side, neither of which is mine, although it is my name too . . ."

After meditating a little on the obscure mysteries of migration, he added that even his grandfather, Constantin's, had the same first and last name as he, Constantin, as his father, Constantin's, and as that uncle of mine, except the initial between the first and last names of his grandfather, Constantin's, which name he, Constantin, didn't know, because he couldn't know it. But he knew for sure that his grandfather had departed a hundred-odd years ago from the splendid mountains that can be seen at the horizon of Ohrid toward the land of the Carpathians where people spoke a fraternal language, "he left to escape the Ottoman yoke," that's how Constantin expressed himself.

When I remarked that my grandfather had left at about the same time the splendid mountains that can be seen at the horizon of Ohrid, apparently to escape being grazed to death by the sheep, Constantin concluded: "How about that! They had no inkling of each other and they met in the cemetery like us, back then, in the newspaper, or like now, on the street . . ."

*A patient who had been suffering from amnesia for 30 years died in a Boston hospital. In spite of numerous announcements published during this period of time, no one claimed him.

12. We remained for a long time there at the corner of Batiştei Street. We were just talking. We both felt that it wasn't possible anymore, that everything was happening for the last time. Perhaps Constantin had truly died, and he was constructing an alibi, that was his business . . .

As far as I was concerned, I would have talked about anything with anybody to dispel the cobweb of our common loneliness. At first I smiled. Truth to tell, only physically, facially (for some time now I had developed the habit of doing so every night before going to sleep and every morning before waking up; the difficulty of this simple but efficient exercise consisted only in knowing when you were asleep and when you could consider yourself awake, given the illusory nature of those two states). Then I decided to laugh. Constantin laughed too, we both chuckled like two madmen, at the corner of Batiştei Street, before the eternal and final leave-taking.

"I'm doing fairly well," said Constantin. "I work at the Revenue Office in Pantelimon township . . ."

"You're somebody . . . !" I leaned against the wall. I wanted to smoke a cigarette.

"I'm in Indirect Taxes," said Constantin. "Do you realize? It's like a dream . . ." (He puffed out his skinny chest.) "I have a nice colleague too, he's going to retire in two months, until then we carry on together, we talk right past the taxpayers, you have no idea how sharp he is. He's much older too . . ."

Something like a little gray puppy, maybe a rat, had stopped near his left foot, it yelped, it sniffed his shoe. There, in the olfactory universe of that cur, something important, it seems, was going on, about which nobody would ever know anything . . .

"He likes me," said Constantin, and I didn't know anymore whether he was talking about his colleague or the rat-dog. "He likes me because I'm ugly, he even told me: 'You are Apollo turned into a turtle to unite with the nymph Dryope,' he said. That's what I am to him, Apollo . . ."

"It may be," I said, just to say something, and I laughed rather inappropriately. Constantin laughed too. The rat-dog had taken off down Batiştei Street.

*Thousands of giant rats attacked three villages in western Java, destroying the rice paddies and silos. The population ran frightened into their homes.

13. Something like a bird passed between us, I heard its fluttering.

"They're all the same," Constantin said, and I didn't know anymore whether he was talking about the bird or Dryope. "In my opinion, there is no difference between them . . ."

He imitated the gestures and the tone of voice of someone else, he affectedly uttered someone else's words, he raised each eyebrow in turn, he pursed his lips. He wasn't laughing anymore.

"You're a hell of a guy . . ." I said.

"It's true," confirmed Constantin. "I peek through the

keyhole from a dark room into the pitch-darkness of the next room. Too bad I can't see much . . ."

"What else do you expect to see?" I laughed in a forced way. I had descended into his hole. "Isn't that enough?"

"Wait, let me explain!" persisted Constantin. He had raised his right index finger. He looked annoyed. "Let me give you an example . . . Six years ago I was serving in the army, in Giurgiu. I knew nobody in the city. On Sundays I walked alone on the banks of the Danube, as far away as possible from the barracks. I wanted to hear some civilian words . . . On one of those Sundays I had wallowed in the Danube and I was drying off stretched out in the weeds when a barge passed by. It was sailing toward the sea. On the deck, a girl was washing laundry in a white basin. I looked at her, I felt how she burned me, like the sun, from a distance, even though she was blonde. When she saw me naked on the bank, she took her hands full of suds from the basin and started to gesture to me. I couldn't resist. I put my hands to my mouth and I started to shout to her, something like this . . ."

And Constantin started to shout terrible obscenities right there, at the corner of Batiştei Street, I won't repeat them. I'll say only that the passersby, rare enough at that time, thinking us drunk, gave us a wide berth, some cursed us too. The rat-dog had returned at a gallop, it thought it had been called. It stuck to Constantin's left shoe, which it sniffed attentively.

"Didn't understand a thing," sighed Constantin, and I didn't know anymore whether he was talking about the cur or that girl on the barge. "She couldn't possibly understand: it was a foreign barge, with an Austrian flag . . ."

Constantin stopped for an instant to caress the head of the cur, which yelped happily.

"Then I got the idea of going to the sea, at least for a day, to look for that barge," he continued. "I have a friend in Constanţa, Poenaru lives near the mosque, his hair has turned gray even though he's young, because of nerves. I thought of staying overnight at his place. I was afraid that the barge might've remained in Brăila or Galaţi, who knows . . . I got leave from the regiment, I said that my mother was dying, and they let me go from Saturday afternoon till Monday morning . . ."

So the next Saturday, Constantin's solitary Anabasis started.

On his way he bought some food. Provisions: salami, cheese, bread . . .

*A colony of termites has attacked part of the structure of Siena Cathedral, threatening to devour it.

14. He knocked in vain at Poenaru's door. Nobody answered. But since he could hear rhythmic music inside accompanied by a metallic clacking, he went in.

Poenaru occupied only one room, big enough, with only one divan in it. In one corner, near a gramophone right on the floor, a blonde girl tap-danced desperately. In the opposite corner, another blonde washed something in a white basin. Poenaru rested on the divan. When he noticed Constantin, he got up on his elbows.

"Look who's here!" he said. He looked happy. He invited his guest, using the only Bulgarian words that he knew: "*Ya la tuka!*"

As if bewitched, Constantin sat down next to him, on the divan. He couldn't take his eyes off the white basin and the blonde who was washing.

"Hey, girls!" shouted Poenaru. "This is my friend from Bucharest . . ."

The blonde with the gramophone pretended not to hear him. The other one only turned her head for a moment and said: "Some ugly friends you have . . . !"

"Don't pay any attention to her," Poenaru tried to excuse her. Then he thought that it was the right moment to make introductions: "The one with the gramophone is Mia, my girlfriend, she's an artist. At night I take her to the cabaret, I stay with her to protect her . . . The one doing the washing is her sister Lilly. She's an artist too, they tap-dance together . . ."

"I know her," mumbled Constantin.

"It's possible," conceded Poenaru. "Lilly is a nice girl too. It's just that she likes to fool around . . . She's staying with us for the time being, till she finds herself a place . . ."

After a while, Constantin brought out the package of provisions. He had gotten hungry. The girls suddenly interrupted their activities. Mia stopped the gramophone, Lilly left her basin. Both of them rushed to the food. They bolted it down in a frenzy. Poenaru sliced the salami, the bread, he took a share for himself. Constantin didn't even get a bite.

Then the girls got ready for the cabaret, and they left with Poenaru. Constantin felt tired, he didn't want to go, he stretched out on the divan.

. . . It seemed to him that he saw a wonderful barge decorated with lights, wreaths, and ribbons in every color sailing through the room. On deck, Lilly was waiting for him, near her white basin, with outstretched arms. The entire scene reminded him of the first meeting between Dante and Beatrice on the bridge, the way he had seen it long ago, in his childhood, printed on a coffee cup made in Sweden. Back then, the poet's terrifying ugliness consoled him: it seemed to him that Alighieri was smoking his nose . . .

When the others came back long after midnight, Constantin was dozing off. Poenaru shook him lightly by the shoulders.

"Wake up," he said. "I sleep on the divan with Mia. You go sleep on the floor, with Lilly . . ."

*Three years before giving birth to octuplets, Pasqualina Chianese had given birth to sextuplets, none of whom survived.

15. It was late. Above Batiştei Street an immense, hostile, yellow moon shone.

"I loved her," said Constantin.

A deep sadness caressed his cheeks. I felt a strange attraction-repulsion to him, a kind of painful pity that I wanted to push away. I thought of Zenobia. Was she asleep or was she waiting for me? When she was a little girl, her mother used to sleep next to her on full-moon nights. She would hold Zenobia's hand tight so she couldn't go away . . . One winter, someone gave her a pair of ice skates as a present. Zenobia struggled in vain for days on end to try and use them. She would fall like a log every time. But one night when there was an immense, round moon like tonight's, she removed her hand from the maternal grasp, put on the ice skates, and went out. When her mother woke up, she saw her ice-skating asleep in the yard, dressed only in a little nightgown. You might have said that she floated, that she flew through the bitter cold, under the trees sparkling with white frost. After that night, she put on the ice skates many times when awake but she was incapable of taking even one step . . .

Nervousness had seized me. During such a phase of the moon I should have been next to Zenobia, to hold her hand tight . . .

"I loved her for six years," said Constantin, "but she didn't love me even for a second. You can't imagine what that was like . . ."

Maybe he feels like becoming melodramatic and he found me, I thought, or maybe he's dead and only his shadow lying in mud and excrement wants to open the gate of promiscuity for me. A nasty dead man, in any event, because the other seen or unseen ones, when they want to make me understand a little of what is only whispered in the ear, content themselves with shaking their heads, serenely and affectionately . . .

"If you feel like crying on my shoulder," I told him, "make sure you don't wet my shirt."

The skin of his face and hands had turned green. A

gloomy green with shades of blue, like that of forests seen from afar.

"You smart-ass!" he grumbled.

I didn't think I was smart. The culpability of intelligence urged me, even back then, to prefer innocence to stupidity.

"Let's talk about something else," I proposed.

"No, no," objected Constantin, "let's keep talking about love . . ."

"If you want," I consented. "Go ahead . . ."

*The scientist Ronald Siegel identified 18 animal species that ingest substances that, while devoid of any nutritional value, have narcotic or hallucinogenic effects.

16. "Love," said Constantin, "is the topic of choice in our conversations at the Revenue Office. You should know that the Old Man furiously rejects any idea of succession. Nothing flows, he states, everything falls, here and now, motionless everywhere and forever. He also maintains that we've been witnessing for thousands of years, unconsciously and impotently, the masculinization of the sacred. I won't go into details because I didn't quite understand his theory, even though he makes every effort to be as clear as possible. I believe it's about a general epidemic that only changes its aspect from time to time. We Europeans were infected by ancient Greece, he says. But there is great hope for change, and a quick one: soon we will all be cretinized by the treacherous intermediary of the spoken, written, and mostly thought word. Until then, each and every one does his best to cretinize himself with the aid of mathematics . . ."

"Not at all stupid, the old man," I judged, wondering why I was still listening to him.

"I told you he was good . . . ! But he is also wrong at times because he's senile. For instance, he believes that for some millennia now we've been witnessing the clinical death of love, and that, also since then, the whole world has gone crazy, everyone sleeps with everyone else but loves only himself. Even in my case, he says that it couldn't be a matter of love, that I've never loved. Just think! I! I never loved . . . ! His opinion is that at present the only constant, the only point that human pseudoloves have in common, and that point is conceived of and treacherously sustained pro and con by an entire spiritual police, is the belief that love can finally entail only unhappiness. Here I'm at a loss, I can't contradict him, he cites examples too . . ."

And Constantin started to enumerate the long string of love's great victims, from Orpheus and Eurydice to Atalanta and Milanion, to Daphnis, Iphis, Ceyx and Alcyone, to the wronged Medea, to Ariadne, to Procris and Cephalus, to Hero and Leander, to Phyllis, Pyramus and Thisbe, to all the Juliets, Ophelias, Margaretas, and Kareninas with all their departed kind on the stage or in books, finally, the entire cohort of those unhappy exemplars who were murdered or who committed suicide because of love.

"There are still plenty of others, but I forget their names," he said. "The Old Man maintains that there is no hint of love in any of these cases. True, he admits, there are exceptions, you can count them on the fingers of one hand, a couple here and there for a few million people, they're pitiful by comparison. They are poor wretches, they live in seclusion in who-knows-what remote places, they make love in their huts until the gods visit them. Then they become trees, that's all they get out of this . . . He considers them the chosen ones, the preservers of love in the world . . ."

"And what if he's not wrong?" I asked casually.

"Do you think you're a chosen one too, by any chance?" Constantin whispered to me. He was almost glued to me, he nearly breathed in my ear.

"I don't give a damn whether I'm a chosen one or not, for your information," I answered and I pushed his face away with the palm of my hand. I even squeezed it a little with my fingers.

"Then let's continue," said Constantin. He had moved aside a little. He seemed resigned again. "Let's consider, for instance, Abelard . . . No, better yet, let's consider my case. Do you know how the story with Lilly ended?"

*A Brazilian pilot, having heard that his wife, Angela, was in the Hotel Barra dos Garcos (Matto Grosso) and suspecting that she had come there for an affair, dove into the hotel building with the twin-engine airplane that he piloted, causing the death of seven people. His wife escaped unharmed.

17. Last autumn, sometime in September, Constantin left unexpectedly for Constanța. He missed Lilly. During the whole trip across the Bărăgan plain down to the sea he floated in a fairylike dream in which only the two of them existed. He was determined not to leave her again, to take her with him forever.

Lilly had long since moved out of Poenaru's place. She lived near the port in a little room separated from the rest of the house, formerly a summer kitchen with clay floor and peeling walls. Constantin went in without knocking. He knew that Lilly never locked the door. He wanted to surprise her.

After the light of the blazing sun outside he perceived next to nothing in the half-dark room. A deep, black silence buzzed in his ears. But to the left he vaguely intuited the shape of the tin washstand. He knew it was painted green and had spots of rust . . . Then he noticed the white basin and the chair full of rags, to which he didn't pay any attention.

Soon the shadowy room grew clearer. His eyes got used to the dim light that managed to pass through the newspaper sheets glued over the windowpanes. Then he looked toward the bed.

From there, from between the sheets, Lilly, silent and immobile, watched him. Beside her, a young man who looked as if he'd just escaped from adolescence stared at him. Constantin saw him clearly, as if he were all of a sudden surrounded by a luminous halo. He saw the lively sparkle in his narrow greenish eyes, he saw his copper-colored hair, he saw his thin collarbones, he even saw the faint shadows of his ribs. The boy had risen to his knees, he waited tensely for the moment when he could grab his clothes and run. His trousers, cotton socks, and boots lay on the floor, near the bed.

Constantin looked at him, dazed. An immense sorrow sank his heart. He wanted to cry, to die, to get it over with . . .

"Get out . . . !" he heard Lilly shout. "Beat it . . . !"

She spoke calmly, in a sharp, unbearable voice. Constantin wanted to smash her mouth in so he wouldn't have to hear her anymore. He looked for something to hit her with. He turned to the chair and saw the rags on it: the redhead's thick linen shirt, his cap, his uniform jacket with its corporal's stripes, the brand-new courier bag of heavy yellow leather with a big lock, the belt with the bayonet attached to it . . .

The redhead jumped from the bed, pulled on his trousers, put on his boots with amazing speed. Constantin seized the belt, he carefully, attentively, wrapped his fingers around the handle of the bayonet. It seemed to him that the handle was hot.

The redhead came close to him, apparently he wanted to get his uniform jacket and the other stuff. "Don't hit me," he said. "It's not my fault. She picked me up on the street, she propositioned me. How could I know that she was a married woman?"

Constantin didn't hear him. He stood stock-still. Before him something unbelievable was happening: he slowly pulled the bayonet from its sheath and its incandescent blade spread flames. It seemed to be made of fire, like the swords of the archangels painted on the walls of churches. Except the flames were black . . .

THE LAST MEETING OF DANTE AND BEATRICE

135

For a moment he looked around madly. Then as fast as he could he pushed the handle back in and threw down the belt, bayonet and all.

The redhead picked it up and put it on. He had put on his uniform jacket, had found his cap and courier bag. For a moment it seemed to Constantin that he didn't have the bayonet anymore. "Maybe he put it inside his bag," he thought.

The redhead turned to Lilly. "I have the honor of saluting you," he said to her.

"Out, you horrible men, both of you, out . . . !" she shouted.

They left together.

In the street, the redhead told him that his name was Semiaza, G. Vasile, that he was from Zalău, and that he would like a beer. Constantin hardly heard him. He was wondering where that G. came from, the initial between the last and first names of the courier corporal.

"I still don't know," he said. "Maybe from Gherasim or Gheorghe, maybe from God . . ."

He didn't have time to tell me what happened afterward on that September afternoon because right then the rat-dog released his foot and started to sniff my right shoe.

"Get away!" I shouted, I was disgusted, I couldn't bear it touching me. I kicked it. It moved aside, yelping.

Perhaps at the same time I unwittingly struck Constantin in the ankle.

"If you chase me away, I'll go," he said sadly and humbly. He bent over in pain. He left. It seemed to me that he carried that rat-dog puppy in his mouth . . .

*As soon as Taro, an eight-year-old dog from the Japanese island of Hokkaido, smells cigarette smoke, it starts wagging its tail happily, its mouth waters, and it starts to follow the smoker. When the latter throws away the cigarette butt, Taro puts it out with a paw and swallows it with great relish. Taro can also pick up the smell of sake from far away; if offered a cup, the dog drinks it on the spot.

18. I experienced the sensation of a dry and sterile annihilation. It was like a fall deprived even of fear, a kind of brutal, opaque, hard-to-explain saturation. A vast renunciation, not mine but the Totality's. Something like a memory buried deep inside me tried in vain to suggest that perhaps it wouldn't take long . . .

Late, in the streets of the city, the seen and, mostly, the unseen people, known or unknown, circled me, attracted by my pitiful state. And each wanted to send me a sign, a word, or at least a name.

First Agrippa with his ambiguous joke. A sign of failure, uncertain like all signs but enough to shake all the reeds that had grown in me. Then, as if by accident, Jason. (Did Petru leave or is he still lamenting at the door in the corridor?) And the girl on the barge with her white basin, and Poenaru with his jovial invitation like a wolf's grin: *"Ya la tuka . . ."* And Mia tap-dancing endlessly, and Lilly (I pitied Lilly), and Semiaza with his bayonet of flames . . . Why did the nameless Old Man from Indirect Taxes convey to me his opinions on the state of love . . . ?

From one to another and from each to each. From the long string of lovers that has been recited to us for centuries, in a loud voice, to the fierce parable of Abelard . . . And who, hidden and pressed in among the rest, tries to lead the game, himself driven, without knowing it, by the rigorous order of the Other Side?

And that Constantin, that monster, that squalid herald, that messenger of promiscuity, what does he want from me? Doesn't he know that I'm still that unfortunate man in the photograph on the yellowed newspaper page? The books have fallen from under my arm, the crown of leaves has wilted, and nobody recognizes me anymore . . .

*About 60 miles from Rome, Biagio di Crescenzio, a 23-year-old man, crashed his car into a tree. After being taken by another car to the hospital in Fondi, the doctors sent him to a clinic in the capital, the only clinic specializing in the kind of surgery that he needed. A couple of miles from the clinic, his ambulance crashed into another vehicle. He was put in another car to be taken to the hospital, and this one crashed into a car coming from the opposite direction. This last crash caused Crescenzio's death and wounded five other people.

19. I headed home, the moon had disappeared. I was thinking of Zenobia. I tried to recalibrate, at least in my mind, the fragility of our relationships with a world of suddenly hostile forces, to protect her from dangers . . .

. . . At the age when other children barely prattled their first syllables, Zenobia talked amazingly well. Except that she substituted some words, especially names of animals, "pig," for instance, with names of her own invention. The others—parents, relatives, neighbors—pleased by her unusual precociousness, made fun, of course, every time she used her invented vocabulary. Soon the little girl felt hurt, she thought that they were making fun of her and from then on she didn't utter a word. For two years running the doctors tried to cure her muteness. Then one day the little girl started to speak on her own again, as fluently as before. Except that since that day she thought her words but uttered the words of others, like some mature people are forced to think in their own language while speaking in another one . . .

Zenobia was very little back then. She's still little now. Maybe I hurt her feelings by leaving her alone for so long and she will become mute again . . .

What was she doing now? Maybe she's sleeping, or maybe she's talking in her thought-language and I don't hear her anymore. Or maybe she realized that I'm a silly, vain person who considers himself chosen because he found himself a few times, by accident, in the lowlands of the Other Side . . . Anyway, Zenobia is very little, tonight I should have stayed home beside her, holding her hand.

I started to run. In the building the elevator didn't work.

I ran up the stairs. I stopped to catch my breath in the corridor. I was panting. Petru had left, apparently, long ago. The yellow glow of the light bulb blended with the gray of dawn.

The door to our room was open. I clearly saw the chair full of dusty papers and the empty divan. In the air I felt an emptiness that added to the emptiness inside me.

"Zenobia," I shouted, "where are you?" I was seized by panic even though I still vaguely hoped that this was a game of hers, that she had hidden, as if in jest . . .

I went into the corridor. The big French window onto the terrace was open. I crossed the threshold. And I remained stock-still.

On the thin tin eaves I saw Zenobia sitting calmly. She swung her legs above the void like a little girl on a swing. She sat with her back turned to me, maybe she didn't see me. Down there, in the abyss below her, the first streetcars rattled, you could see the morning's first passersby. The rather flimsy eaves could have broken and collapsed at any second.

"Zenobia!" I managed to say (I was out of breath). "Don't move! I'm coming to get you . . ."

But I couldn't move at all. I felt as if I were wearing lead boots nailed to the floor.

She turned around calmly, passed one leg over the other (I saw her as if I were just a step away), jumped onto the terrace, and came to me.

"I was afraid," she said, "I was afraid that something might have happened to you . . ."

I took her in my arms, she was incredibly light. I went back through the window with her. She had pressed her forehead to my cheek, she was very little and round, like that ball of rays that she had drawn next to my ear the evening of Dragoş's departure. I hardly dared breathe for fear that she might dissolve.

"You didn't behave," she whispered.

"Zenobia," I said, "don't you ever do this again, understand? If this happens again, I'll die, believe me, I will . . ."

VI

■ □ ■ □ ■

THE WITNESSES

1. EACH PERSON CARRIES WITHIN AN UNTRUTH MEANT TO explain the tangled movement of the sublunary world. This is called truth, and it lasts until another truth appears. Its destiny seems to be to clash, in turn, first with the aggressive truths of others, taken separately, and then the depressing truth of everyone, taken as a whole.

2. That afternoon it was very hot again. I stayed in the room, stretched out on my back, I was meditating, when the Visitor appeared.

She was a large, stout woman. As I looked her over from toe to head, she resembled a hulk. She wore a little white piqué hat with the brim turned up on one side, she had bangles too, you would have thought that she had just got out from behind the wheel of an ancient Ford convertible. She rested her palms against the frame of the wide-open door and stared at me. I had never seen her but I could swear that she was Maria's mother.

"Are you Naum?" she asked.

I could have said no and gotten away but because I wasn't in the habit of lying, I said yes and stood up. I hardly fit between the wall and the sofa.

"There's not enough room here," I explained to her (I was stammering), "but I'll remove the chair . . ."

I cleared away all the stuff that was on the chair, dusted it off nicely with my sleeve, and took it out into the corridor. It was hot there too, the light bulb was still on, ugly and yellowish, like a light smothered by light. I placed the chair near the bathroom. She sat down, dignified and menacing.

"Where is Maria?" she asked. She was curt and authoritarian. She held her purse tight on her knees.

I was crouched on the floor in Petru's lamentation space. I sat still, being careful not to transgress its limits, even by a fraction of an inch.

"I don't know," I answered. "She dropped by only once, and I wasn't home then."

"Don't lie to me!" the Visitor warned. Now I clearly saw her slightly wilted cheeks, the soft outline of her chin, the wrinkle between her eyebrows. She spoke rather rudely to me, I could have pulled that little piqué hat over her eyes. She was rummaging in her purse, she was looking for something in there . . .

*At the Nairobi airport, a Boeing 747 with 361 passengers aboard ran into a hyena, and the flight had to be canceled.

3. "You must tell me where she is," she continued. "You must know . . ."

I explained to her that between Maria and me there had never been what she imagined. It's true, I had lived for some time in her studio with my fiancée because we didn't have a home, but even then I saw Maria rather seldom, there was nothing between us, I swear, we were only friends . . .

The Visitor frowned less at me, maybe she felt that I wasn't lying. She took an awfully white handkerchief from her purse and wiped the corner of her right eye. She informed me that Maria had disappeared two weeks ago. Someone (she didn't tell me who, but I immediately thought of Ioachim) had advised her to stop by my place and had even given her the address . . .

"Put yourself in my situation," she tried to justify herself.

"If your own daughter had disappeared, and after stealing money from the house . . ."

She was afraid that Maria could have committed some *irreparable* foolishness.

"She's crazy," she said, "and there are so many hooligans out there . . ."

I told her that it was true, I myself knew a few, but some were very likable. Besides, boys and girls usually make love. Sometimes (very seldom) they even love each other. Maybe Maria fell in love and then . . .

"Maria fall in love? You don't know her . . . She's completely devoid of any feelings . . ."

Now we talked like friends. From somewhere, from I don't know which floor, an Unknown meddled in our conversation, he started a gramophone, you could hear it fairly well. The Visitor fell silent. She had covered her eyes with the handkerchief. It seemed to me that she sighed.

*A fire caused by the violent crash between a truck carrying chickens and another truck carrying steak sauce resulted in the frying of hundreds of chickens scattered on the highway among the jars of sauce, the wounding of several people, and the stopping of traffic for several hours.

4. I left her like this for a while. I had the impression that she was burying me in sand.

"Lady," I said then, because I didn't know her first name, "there's a fly on your stocking."

I wondered how that fly had reached as high as our apartment.

She shooed the fly away, then looked at me. She was frowning again. She regretted her moment of weakness. She regrouped under cover of a didactic dignity. Maybe she was haunted by the routine of teaching. Anyway, she resumed talking. She uttered only stern phrases, she was flattening my brain. I was expecting her to ask me about Hegel. She proved to me verbally, with unassailable arguments, that the only real and omnipotent feeling that nature itself dictates as such, lifting it out of the dark pit of instincts, is maternal love, and so on.

I listened to her in silence. In order to put up with her, in my mind I gave her a pair of big, Cossack-like mustaches. She looked good with them.

At one point, she stopped to breathe.

"Lady," I said, "you are perfectly right. I know the feeling myself. It had always impressed me, even though I was an orphan from an early age, my father died when I wasn't even two years old, so there was nobody to beat me. Only my mother beat me, and I'm convinced that she had feelings . . ."

The Visitor looked at me, confused. She thought I was a cretin, no doubt about it, maybe indeed I was but, to my surprise, she smiled.

"Stop that 'Lady,'" she said. "I don't like it . . ." She spoke softly. She leaned her bust toward me.

At that moment, what I'd been feeling but refused to believe became clear: the Visitor emanated Maria's pervading warmth.

The Unknown had changed the record, now a Charleston was being played. I could see Buster wagging his little tail, it seemed to me that Mrs. Ojog (may she rest in peace) tried to stick her sweaty face against my cheek, although there was still enough space between us.

"Lady," I said, because I couldn't call her anything else, "I always wanted an affectionate and oversized mother like you, but life had other things in store . . . But now I have to retire for a few minutes because I feel an urgent physical necessity . . ."

I stood up and went into the bathroom, leaving her alone to ruminate on that feeling of hers . . .

---

*The most voluminous woman in the world, the 49-year-old English housewife Muriel Hopkins, passed away from a heart attack.

According to some estimates, she weighed over 700 pounds. During the last weeks of her life, Muriel couldn't walk because her legs could no longer support her weight, and she preferred to sleep in a special chair because she couldn't climb into bed anymore.

5. I was sitting on the lid in the dark. I had adopted the pose of the Thinker. I didn't have any physical necessity other than that of being alone. I had a rather crooked smile, I could have cried, I felt like a poor seaman lost in the ocean, in a region of flat and absolute calm. I had been humiliated by the Visitor's canine hermeneutics, which were meant to scorch my bones. I was ashamed of myself. My blabber barely managed to annihilate her. I could still feel her warmth, it seemed to me that she had stuck to the door frame, I feared that she might set it on fire.

So Ioachim had memorized my address and kept his promise, he had sent me his last book, in flesh and blood . . .

In addition to him and Maria, the Visitor, and maybe Jason, the precariousness of my state prevented my verifying the fifth little wheel of the mechanism. But through the mist of revulsion that had seized me I felt vaguely how someone more powerful than they was hammering at my joints.

At the same time, a seemingly foreign and indistinct thought whispered to me that maybe I was being tested . . .

*The owner of a hotel stopped for refreshments at an inn on his way to the bank where he was going to deposit a large sum of money. After sitting near a cow shed and quietly drinking a mug of cider, he noticed that a cow had devoured his money bag.

6. Then I thought, for some reason, of Father. He had died long ago, I had almost forgotten him. I remembered him only when I received his messages. But I'll talk about this only when I feel that it's appropriate to do so.

Anyway, I felt the need for a sign that would shake up my mental virtues a little. And I *heard* Ze Wo asking: "What's the point of observing three years of mourning after one's parents die when a single year would be enough?" He said *three years* although so many had already passed. ("What an insensitive man!" the Master thought.)

"Everything is so stupid," I said to myself. "Maybe I haven't sufficiently prepared myself . . ."

Behind that door I could envision the Inferno. Where had Zenobia gone off to? Of course, she's pasting up letters, she doesn't give a damn about me. She had left me here on purpose, where even Orpheus went wrong. He forgot that because of that he was torn to pieces by the Thracian women . . .

And I thought of Him, three times my gentle brother. I was saying: none of us has the right to despise His weakness. None of us. So let them rest, undisturbed, under the willows, the fragments of bones and flesh of His eternal whole . . .

I could hear the gramophone from behind the door. The same Charleston. And I could actually see our encounter again.

*For 19 months now, in the town of Rogerville (France), a dog has been coming daily to the grave of his former master, pressing his muzzle against the marble of the tombstone and howling with grief. This seems all the more surprising since on the day of the funeral the dog had been locked indoors and couldn't have known where his master was buried.

7. It was dawn, in the field, at the beginning of one autumn. I let the trails guide me. I saw passing in the distance, like heaps of steam, the silent, redeeming women. On their backs they carried large bundles of brushwood and corn-stalks to their hearths. Their haziness threw me into the fog of a perplexing era.

As I walked along, the tracks led me to a shore. There I stopped. And I recognized Him immediately in spite of His lack of magnificence.

He stood on the shore, shivering. He had lost His lyre but He had near at hand, in a spot sheltered from moisture, a violin and a bow.

He appeared to me as a rather dark-skinned, weedy, and pallid adolescent. He wore a wide, old, ultrascrawny frock coat with long tails faded by the sun. He used a crooked reed and a cord made of knitted horsehair. He caught some little white fish that he shoved into the pocket of his frock as you would shove in a pen or a matchbox. In order not to lose the earthworm from the hook, He first slapped it between His palms, He stunned it.

I sat behind Him, on a root. Above, between the branches of the willows, the sky shone.

After a while He became aware that I was there and turned to me. He asked me whether I wanted Him to sing to me. He had left the fishing rod in the water.

I said yes, He took His violin and bow, He accompanied Himself with them, He chanted (with a twang).

A snake and a bird came, they stood near us, they listened and became tame.

I had some money on me, I gave it to Him. The snake and the bird went away. He sat beside me, He felt like talking. He told me that His name was Irina.

"That happens . . ." (I wasn't surprised by His feminine name.)

Then, still talking about this and that, He mentioned the moon. "Yes, the moon is round," He informed me, "but it destroys itself, it's consumed by its own fire until next to nothing remains and it burns again because up there an accursed wind blows, it goes out and rekindles any spark, no matter how little . . ." (He rushed to the fishing rod, He took out a little fish, no bigger than a fingernail, He shoved it into His pocket, and He turned back to me. He smiled, serene and calm.) "Some people say that the earth is round too. What do you think?"

"I don't know," I said, "it's possible but I'm not too sure . . ." Above us the sky had flared up.

"I heard that in Bucharest there is a big whale," He changed the subject. "It's on exhibit at the Moşilor Fair, people from all over come to see it . . ."

"There is one there, in a warehouse, it's dead and stuffed . . ."

"I was wondering, because whales only live in deep water, in oceans . . ." (He started to laugh.) "What would you say if I caught one on this poor hook of mine . . . ?"

He went on to tell me that He had a respiratory illness, and that His wife had died, also of consumption. He told me the story of His marriage. The girl was about fourteen. He had turned eighteen and they agreed that He would come one Sunday night to elope with her. The well-behaved girl told her parents, so that night they went to some neighbors, where they could watch the elopement through the fence. As for Irina, He got a suit, He bought Himself a pair of patent-leather shoes, and He killed a snake with whose skin He covered a stick, "a bridegroom's cane," He said. Then, on Sunday, in the dark, He came with a cart, accompanied by two of His cousins to elope with His bride.

On their way home, after He had eloped with her, He took off his patent-leather shoes because His feet were hot. He walked barefoot beside the cart. The bride maintained that now, since she was His bride, He absolutely had to buy her a doll.

"What do you need a doll for, when you have this large-as-life doll beside you?" joked one of the witness-cousins, the one driving the cart.

Irina rushed to the fishing rod again, He took out of the water a little fish and He shoved it into the bottomless pocket of His frock. After that He didn't sit down anymore. He suddenly became sad.

"She passed away two weeks ago." He considered it necessary to be precise. "I don't have much time to live either. I'll go after her, into the ground, to look for her . . ."

Then He picked up His fishing rod, He hid it in the reeds, He took His violin and bow and He left . . .

*One afternoon, a cloud of butterflies blocked dozens of automobiles on a freeway near Padua. Thousands of butterflies stuck to the windshields of the cars, which had to stop and wait for help. Firefighters and carabinieri sent to the spot restored the flow of traffic.

8. The time required by writing does not coincide with the duration of things narrated here. They unwind between extremes, either with the speed commonly called "of thought" or in slow motion. In this respect, the only exceptions are the bookish phrase of Ze Wo, perhaps uttered by my very mouth, and the excoriated orphic hypostasis.

The only consistent thing was the space that destroyed my idea that I could escape from it: I was in an infinite cage that had its bars outside and inside me.

In that immense horizontal space, without near or far, with the beginning and the end at the same point, appeared Jeni Pop.

I had met her two or three years before. She was a blonde girl who wore an uncommonly long gray dress with fringed sleeves and hem. While talking she made strange gestures, thrusting out her bust, twitching her shoulders, contracting her buttocks. She had picked me up on the street, she wanted us to walk arm in arm and pass in front of a certain house. She told me her whole drama in a few words.

(When she was fourteen, in full bloom and splendor, she fell into a cellar. From then on she didn't have legs, she wore pneumatic prosthetic devices, she described them to me in detail. She said that she was in love with one Nelu Gologan. I knew him, he lived near my place, and she knew he didn't look at her because of the prosthetic devices. She wanted Nelu Gologan to see her going out with boys, she hoped that this would lead to something . . .)

We walked for about two hours, she kept talking about prosthetic devices, I avoided eye contact, I looked upward. It was a painful and useless walk because Nelu Gologan didn't appear. Since that time I've seen her only once, she was passing by on the other side of the street, pushed in a wheelchair. Apparently the prosthetic devices . . .

*Eleven physically handicapped people have begun an ascent of Mount Rainier, 14,410 feet high.

*The Canadians Ron Minor and Ron Payette, 23 and 32 years old, respectively, crossed the Rocky Mountains, covering 680 miles in 15 days. This marathon is an unprecedented world event, since the two young men are handicapped and crossed the mountains in wheelchairs.

9. Now, from the seat, I followed her gestures: she floated in front of me in slow motion, seemingly carried by her long dress. I remind you that we were on the eighth or ninth floor of the high-rise building, but the conversion of the vehicle-space made everything seem to be happening at ground level. Between the pavement, which she floated above without touching, and the fringes of the hem of her dress, I caught a glimpse of the void.

In her long gray dress Jeni Pop performed the floating dance. She was neither far nor close, even though she moved farther out and closer in. She moved farther out, her back turned to me, keeping me near, in the fixed spot where I watched her.

Then, after a last graceful pirouette, she gestured to me, she raised one arm, the left one. I felt on my eyelids the thin fluttering of the fringes of her sleeves, I could hear their rustle too. I closed my eyes . . .

When I opened them it was dark. I could make out something undefined and black in the pitch-darkness. A woman's voice whispered: "Maître, do you have a light . . . ?"

The title surprised me in an unpleasant way. It seemed to me that someone wanted to make jokes at my expense. Then I told myself that perhaps it was not meant to sound sarcastic. Other people, who have nothing in common with pohetry, call each other: "Maître . . ."

I began to see, and near me was the wheelchair of a handicapped woman whose face was lost in the dark.

"Maître!" she felt obliged to repeat while I was looking for the matches.

I lit a match and I stretched my arm out toward the place where I supposed the cigarette was. Then I clearly saw Jeni Pop. She sat motionless in the wheelchair and looked at me.

The match burned my fingers. I tossed the matchbox in her lap.

She lit her cigarette, she smoked it to the end. I stood there dumbfounded, I saw the lit end of the cigarette getting closer and closer to my eyes.

"Maître," Jeni Pop shouted, "I loved him, Maître . . ."

I watched her with a sense of unease, she passed before me in her wheelchair, she didn't wear the fringed dress anymore, she was wrapped in transparent veils, pink, mauve, orange, fluttering. She showed me her navel, her belly . . . She jerked her shoulders to the rhythm of a Charleston that didn't stop for a moment. She screamed, sang, and assaulted my ears and eyes with her ferocious melodrama.

I had only one wish: to stop this obsessive back-and-forth motion. A few inches behind me was the opaque window, full of dust and ashes, of the light well. I turned around and opened it. I leaned over and looked into the void.

From the first instant, depth became horizontal. I pulled back, and then I leaned out the window again. This time a blue searchlight lit the dark to the end. There I saw on the moldy concrete slab a crushed human body in a pool of blood. It had neither form nor face. Something undefinable and sad reminded me of Petru . . .

I wanted to scream but managed to control myself. I felt like throwing up. Then the searchlight went off and I didn't see anything.

When I returned from the window Jeni Pop had disappeared, wheelchair and all. I unbolted the door and came out of the bathroom.

It seemed I had stayed there too long. The Visitor had left. In the corridor was only the stiff and empty chair, like a lonely witness whose testimony no one would have believed.

*Nine cats, which had miniature devices attached to their skulls to record cerebral activity, were stolen from the National Center for Scientific Research in Paris.

10. I ran down the stairs, I couldn't possibly stand the elevator cage. I needed to talk to someone, anyone, about anything, to reestablish in some way the arbitrary common link. I thought of looking for the doorman so we could enter the light well together but I gave up. How could he believe that I had looked from the eighth or ninth floor all the way down through the dark?

On the street, the first person I saw was a pretzel vendor. He had moved into the shade of a chestnut tree, he was hiding from the heat. I bought a pretzel.

Two people stopped near us, an old man (he could hardly drag his feet) and a still-young woman. The woman held in her hand a brand-new wooden spoon.

She bought a pretzel too, she broke off a little piece and gave it to the old man.

"Listen, Father," she said, "I have a pig with one blue eye and one green eye . . ."

"That's beautiful," judged the old man, munching his bite of pretzel.

"Sure. It's like a photograph . . ."

"Don't forget to give her the spoon," said the old man. (He'd finished eating.) "Tell her I bought it for her with my own money . . ."

"You'd better give it to her, I'm on bad terms with her . . ."

The old man took the spoon from his daughter's hand, threw it in the middle of the street, and left mumbling. The young woman made a "he's crazy" gesture, picked up the spoon from the spot where it had landed, and went off in the opposite direction.

"Listen," I asked the pretzel vendor, "do you happen to know what the normal eye color is for pigs?"

"It depends," he answered briefly.

The conversation didn't get off the ground. I was afraid I'd said something wrong. But the pretzel vendor was calmly counting his money, his back turned to me, he didn't pay me any attention.

I left him, I set off walking down the boulevard. Noon had long since passed, but the sun was still shining. I followed people, I kept pace with them, I hobbled like the lame, I panted like the fat, I tried to enter a little into their reality, to forget what I knew about its fragility. In that increasingly hard-to-bear state I almost envied their reassuring certainties.

Some shouted at me, they protected their limits disturbed by my persistent indiscretion. A lady called me an ass, God knows what she imagined, maybe I was indeed an ass.

I tried to explain myself, I mumbled that nothing was like this, that everything was different, that I needed them, the presence of each and every one, and their words, however stupid, to convince myself that we existed together. One of them gave me a shove, I bumped against a wall and fell to the ground. I thought of Zenobia: if she were with me . . .

If she were with me maybe she would have tried to help me, in any event she would have said: "You're a child, really!

Stay calm. All of this is happening to you because you're climbing one more step. I know it's hard but I can't do anything about it. Try to behave . . ."

I felt like yelling: "Why are you leaving me, Zenobia? I know what you can do and what you can't. Better yet, to hell with all those steps! How many of them are there till the end when we become dust and ashes? How long will I torment myself? For your information, I don't give a damn about those steps and circles and their ups and downs. I've had enough. For your information, it's not hard—it's *terrible* like this, on your own, I know the trick: someone inside me is leading me around. I am my own projection, a cretin who doesn't want to get anywhere for anything . . . And you keep talking about my behaving myself and reining myself in to be free . . ." I felt like laughing: "For your information, you're right. I've been talking like this to comfort myself . . ."

*A huge herd of baboons invaded a plantation in northern Somalia, starting a real battle. The apes threw stones at people who tried to block their way, then they started hand-to-hand combat. The fierce battle that lasted for two days resulted in 363 apes dead and 6 people gravely wounded.

11. I lay still. The witnesses were already gathering, some maintained that the first-aid should be called.

"He's all right," said the one who had shoved me. "He's drunk or crazy. I hardly touched him. He lost his balance. Can't you see? He's quite sturdy . . ."

Actually, I could have gotten up very easily, greeted them most respectfully, and scurried home, but it was good down there, on the asphalt, with my eyes closed. I played a pleasant game: between the imagined imaginary and the lived imaginary I was tempted by the nostalgia of a possible paradise. I found it again in two hypostases, both lost in the not-too-distant fogs of childhood. (I'm talking about a state and not about landscapes or existential facts . . .)

In the first one I was at a mill on the Teleajen River, at Uncle Vitu's house, a cousin of my father's. My mother had sent me to stay with him one summer, when I was about four years old, to relieve the household budget, which was still anemic enough. The river was often high there and flooded its banks. Then I would stay inside the mill as if in an ark smelling of flour. Sometimes, at night, Uncle Vitu fished with a trident in the pond by torchlight. When the waters retreated, carts brought flour to grind. Hares would sneak up behind them, they ate the grain that spilled from the sacks. Maybe it was my imagination but I, who knew how to stop rains when they were too boring, actually saw them, and I played with them . . .

The second hypostasis took me, when I was about six, to the Terra movie theater on Doamnei Street. I could read perfectly, I wrote lines of poetry too. Nothing meritorious in all this, maybe the contrary.

Half the Terra was taken up by the balcony. That's where the tough guys from the outskirts of Bucharest hung out, they were illiterate and generous, ever ready to use their knives. They sat on the floor, smoked, clapped their hands, and cursed. Among them I imagined myself the lonely cowboy lost in the canyons. I dismounted, went into a saloon . . .

They all knew me: I read the titles of the movies to them, I explained things to them when they didn't understand. They paid for my ticket. During intermissions, they spoiled me, they bought me candy, chocolate, caramels, waffles, cherries in rum . . . They considered me as one of their own in an ample and serene fraternity. Like them, I always took the side of the girl. (Oh, how I loved her, each and every time . . .)

*Thirty-three-year-old Charlotte Mottinger was held in captivity for two decades by her 61-year-old mother. This discovery was made by accident at a routine checkpoint. Charlotte was tied to the back seat in an uncomfortable position, she had injuries to the head, and her mental development was arrested at the adolescent level.

12. After that, the reverie bored me. I pushed away a couple of compassionate people who were leaning over me, I sprang to my feet and took flight. The witnesses were stunned for a moment, then they started to run after me. Others joined them. A great uproar began, they shouted as loud as they could: "Get him . . . !"

A streetcar was coming toward me, I jumped on the steps, the witnesses remained behind. I saw how they were losing ground. Soon they gave up and stopped shaking their fists . . .

I entered a car that was almost empty. The few passengers, old men and women, sat quietly, the palms of their hands resting on their knees. If I hadn't seen the houses parading on each side of the street, I could have imagined myself in a classroom full of students suddenly grown old. A strange silence reigned in the car. Nobody talked, everyone looked off to the side.

From the first moment I realized that something unusual was going on there. The few passengers who dared to get off at the stops sneaked to the exit door as if to the gates of a cemetery. New passengers immediately joined the game: they sat down quietly on the empty seats and were silent. A feeling of respectful sadness, a calm and exhausted desolation, floated above them.

I stopped at the rear of the car and I watched. It took me a while to realize the cause of the passengers' strange behavior.

At the other end of the car was a man in his thirties, the only person standing. He appeared to be an unnaturally natural bearer of the natural, if I can put it this way. A champion of normality. He was dark, with a common face, small and stout, wearing a fairly proper suit, you could have taken him for a honest worker, maybe a plumber, needed somewhere for a job that he would perform as he was expected to.

That man was motionless too, but in profile, turned slightly to the right. He looked calmly out the window. Naturally, he would have passed unnoticed if he hadn't, from time to time, turned his head extremely slowly toward the others. Then they guiltily lowered their eyes, sad and seemingly embarrassed by their own existence.

He wasn't trying to dominate but he did so by his calm passivity. He thought it normal for those people to keep their eyes lowered, and he looked at them with understanding and compassion.

When he turned his face to the interior of the car a second time, I noticed a detail that I had missed at first glance: the man wore thin wire-rimmed glasses with no lenses. Their subtle and necessary presence was justified by the fact that he added, where the bridge rests on the nose, a second nose, parallel to his own, made of silver foil or tinfoil and glued on like some people glue a leaf, when sunbathing, to protect their peeling noses from the sun. Except that his leaf looked like a duckbill and stretched out stiffly above the first nose without touching it.

In addition he wore in his hatband a little ornamental feather (like hunters do) made of newspaper skillfully cut with scissors.

Every time that man turned his head, the funerary color of his silver nose shone dimly like candlelight over a dead man, causing in the surrounding people, along with the mediocre satisfaction that *they were normal,* an intense melancholy.

When the man noticed me, he smiled gently and greeted me by raising one finger. I greeted him, also with one finger, and I jumped off the streetcar. I had reached home at Romană Square.

*From aboard a helicopter, Yvon Yva succeeded in putting 15 people to sleep in 30 seconds in front of an audience of 5000 gathered in the Municipal Conference Center in Quebec. This mass hypnosis lasted for 50 hours and 26 minutes.

13. It was still hot upstairs. The sun's red light shone at an angle through the dusty windows of the corridor. While I

was gone someone had turned off the light bulb, someone had moved the chair from where I had left it. I thought of Zenobia. Maybe she had come home earlier than usual and was waiting for me . . .

I stopped in front of the bathroom and went in to look one more time in the light well. Nothing, except the usual darkness. (I mumbled: "Why do they call it a light well, this space of perpetual darkness . . . ?")

The chair was in the room, in its place. On it I found a note from Zenobia: "I'll be waiting for you at the movie theater." That was all. Neither what time nor what movie theater.

I washed and rested a little. Then when I felt that the time had come, I set off at random. I took a streetcar, then a bus, that light guided me . . . I found myself in a neighborhood where I hadn't been in a long time. I came across a movie theater that I hadn't heard of before. Zenobia was waiting for me at the entrance holding two tickets in her hand. She said: "It starts at seven . . ." It was five minutes to seven.

We went in. We weren't surprised, either of us . . .

*Koichi Oguri, of Tateyama, Japan, succeeded in growing a lily that was 10 feet high and had 141 blossoms.

14. Back home, I told Zenobia what had happened during the day; I had to. She listened to me without saying a word. (I wished she would say something.) When I was done she went to the light well *to see*. She quickly returned. She seemed tired and sad.

"Relax," she said. "Nothing's happened yet . . ."

Then she went to sleep.

I stretched out beside her on the sofa. I couldn't sleep. I couldn't keep my mind off Petru.

Late at night, it seemed to me that I heard something like a thud or a stifled groan. I got up and walked over to the light well again. A band of light hovered in front of the second window below us, forming a curtain almost like steam. Beyond it, the darkness looked even darker.

Back in the room I stretched out again beside Zenobia. I felt enveloped by her deep calm and I tried to calm down.

I tossed and turned for a long time until I heard Petru's lament. Then I felt relieved: that meant that he was alive . . . Down there, if I really had seen something, lay someone else . . .

In the numbness that had seized me I realized, however, that his lamentations were shorter than on other nights. "He might have gotten bored," I said to myself, "or maybe he realized . . ."

That was the last night I heard him. After that, Petru disappeared forever from my life.

*Peter Snyman, a 26-year-old carpenter, emerged from a cage of poisonous snakes at the Hartebee-Spoort Zoo near Johannesburg, where he had remained for 50 days.

15. When I went out in the morning to buy bread, I found Petru's mat in front of our door. Usually, he took it with him. I told myself that maybe he'd left it with us, who knows, or maybe Zenobia had found it when she'd left and she had moved it to our door to attract my attention . . .

Out in front of the building a few people had gathered, they talked about a girl's suicide. The doorman recounted, who knows how many times, the story of how he had found her crushed on the cement when he had gone to clean the light well.

As usual on such occasions, people argued passionately and a lot of details were mentioned. So I found out that the girl was sixteen, that she was crippled in both legs, and that she lived with her father, the attorney Persu, in an apartment two stories below our corridor. An imaginary plumb line starting from Nathalia's empty room would have reached her bedroom exactly.

The witnesses were particularly curious about how the young handicapped girl, without legs and without her wheelchair, which was left near her bed, could have reached the light well window.

"She crawled," a woman tried to explain. "I know because I worked in their house. The young lady never went to the bathroom. She used the chamber pot in her bedroom . . ."

And she described in detail the intimate procedures of the deceased.

To me, the strangest thing in their commentaries was the fact that none of them uttered the first name of the girl: they called her "the dead person" or "the lawyer's daughter" or "Miss Persu."

As far as I was concerned, even though I avoided thinking of the more or less demented link that could just as well have existed or not between Petru's nocturnal lamentations, my visions, and the tragic suicide of an unknown girl, I was convinced from the outset that her first name could only have been Nathalia . . .

*A pressed rose that Greta Garbo had offered with a kiss as a present was sold at auction . . .

16. From that morning on things calmed down. The nightmare of the intermediary state had suddenly dissipated. Something necessary, in which I had let myself be unconsciously implicated, though against my will, had been carried out.

I knew to what extent everything was favored by my almost unnoticed errors of behavior too. "I knew" is a manner of speaking. Actually, I intuited only a few, poor, successive—and at the same time random—effects situated in an area without direction, whose wretched immediate elements were usually treacherous.

Actually, I knew that I didn't want to know *like this;* actually, I foresaw a subapparent movement whose final point contained the beginning too. Actually, I intuited the final point everywhere and especially in the rigorous free zone beyond it. Actually, I intuited it in a reversible way up to nonexistence, I can't be clearer because I always speak of something else.

Actually, I wasn't interested either in understanding or in explaining. I knew without knowing, by a logic of states that is difficult to express and difficult to understand for those situated outside it . . .

*In New Delhi, an Indian airplane hit a vulture and was forced to land.

17. I spent the entire day alone. Toward evening I went out into the streets, among the living and dead witnesses of our giant existential farce. Once again I was to play a rather fierce game.

It was growing dark, the sky reddened toward the west, the dead passed by, the fingers of some of them shone, they had no idea of our game.

In front of a pharmacy I intuited a smile like a glimmer in the window. A figure remained there, on the other side of the windowpane. I addressed it as gently as possible: "Good evening, Mrs. Gerda . . ."

"Exthaohdinahy . . . !" she exclaimed. "Imagine, I was thinking of you this vehy second . . ."

"Mrs. Gerda," I said, "you have always been very sensitive and it's no wonder that once in a while you think of me too, *no matter how much time has passed*" (I was humming). "In spite of some controversies due mainly to my unfortunate psychic structure, I dare to believe that, back then, you cared a little about me . . ."

"I cahed foh you like a bhotheh," admitted Mrs. Gerda, blushing slightly; her hair was beautifully peroxided. "And if you hadn't been so—"

"Forbidding, that's the word, Mrs. Gerda, why shouldn't I admit it? *Now I'm sorry, even though it's too late*" (I was humming).

"How time flies!" sighed Mrs. Gerda. "Hehe we ahe, both of us matuhe . . ."

The light was growing dim, Mrs. Gerda shook her head, the dead continued their walk, they passed by us as if in a dream. In the pharmacy powerful blue lights went on, I proposed to Mrs. Gerda that she should come outside, to sit with me on the curb, to discuss discussions. I thought that she might be pleased by a short verbal communion.

"Oh no!" she objected. "What would people think, especially now that I'm mahhied . . . ?"

I pressed my palms and face against the window, my nose was flattened, I wanted to get to the other side, the conversation would have become ennobled. Mrs. Gerda rested just her palms against the other side of the windowpane.

The dead are generally quite nice people, and the pharmacist didn't seem to be an exception, he sat on a white chair, he weighed up something, he didn't pay any attention to us . . .

"Mrs. Gerda," I said, after contemplating her for a few moments, "would it be indiscreet of me to ask who the lucky man is . . . ?"

"He's an eldehly man," she answered, "an old family fhiend but he is vehy hale and heahty, you wouldn't think him mohe than fifty yeahs old . . ."

"Then I congratulate you . . ."

"Oh, thank you . . ."

And so on . . .

*Eighty-two-year-old Plenie Wingos, having hiked backward 800 miles in 1931–1932, is preparing for a new trek. His gear includes, among other things, glasses with rearview mirrors.

18. Then Mrs. Gerda rested her face against the window too, she stuck her mouth to it, she wanted to explain, even though it wasn't necessary. I pulled back a little.

"I was so lonely," she whispered to me. "My motheh had died, you cannot imagine how much I loved heh . . . She was vehy special . . . Too bad you didn't meet heh . . ."

"I met her, Mrs. Gerda, the day before I left that corridor. I didn't have the opportunity to tell you, that's why you didn't know . . ."

"It's neveh too late, " she sighed. "Why don't you tell me the stohy now? You have no idea how much I loved heh . . ."

It was obvious that she wanted to throw me back into the past, and for a moment I thought of resisting.

"Mrs. Gerda," I said, "don't you think it's getting late and about time for us to go home to our own places? At this time of day perhaps someone is waiting for me too, because we're humans not beasts . . ."

"Please!" she insisted.

Without realizing it she had passed halfway through the window, she had leaned her bust out over the street, next to me.

*The Japanese doctor Sadaio Sumide succeeded in bringing back to life the frozen hearts of rats and mice stored for two years at a temperature of −195 degrees centigrade, reactivating them by electric impulses.

19. I sensed the trap, but it was all the same to me. I started to tell her the story. However, I spoke cautiously, I measured my words.

"Before I begin, I would like to ask you something," I said. "Don't remember any of the names that I might mention. You know how it is: say a name and gain a relative . . . Otherwise, I assure you that the bearers of those names had at the most a culthural relationship both to your mother and to yours truly, though they were among the very few that still counted . . ."

Mrs. Gerda listened attentively to me. The dead had

turned joyful, they passed by, they seemed not to see us. The young ones embraced each other.

"So," I resumed, "it was a Friday, toward evening, I had left the door open, I lay stretched out on the floor in my room. A friend had visited me, I voiced my opinion, contrary to his conviction, that pohetry doesn't punctuate action anymore, it's been ahead for a long time." (I was becoming pitiful . . .) "Then someone else had come by, he wanted to persuade me that pohetry had to be made by all. Actually, in spite of the musty old perfume that they emanated, I loved them for their way of life and especially for their way of death . . . Then I don't know why, I found myself face to face with Robespierre (I would have preferred Saint-Just, but he was the one who came). He shouted his speeches into my ears, I had enough, I redid them, he could get angry for all I cared . . .

"So this was the general setting and the data of that moment about which I don't care, now and forevermore, amen, when the first woman's shoe arrived, spinning in the air through the wide-open door and hitting the floor near me. A kind of poltergeist. In your capacity as an Austrian I'm sure you'll understand . . . Besides, I could have sworn that that shoe, so cracked and crooked, was yours . . ."

20. "The second shoe hit me in the head. The two poets, as well as Robespierre, got scared and scurried off. I got up from the floor and went out into the corridor. There was nobody there, but the door to your room was open and from inside one could hear groans, as if someone were in agony. I went in. Stretched out on a heap of newspapers lay your old mother . . .

"'I'm dying!' she announced desperately.

"'Come on,' I said, 'people don't die just like that . . .'

"I gave her the medicine (she was still able to show it to me, her index finger trembled). I brought her a glass of water and remained beside her to see her unfold. I stood like that and looked around the room. I admired the perfect simplicity of the furniture, the exquisite taste in emphasizing the void. As far as I remember there were some more newspapers, freshly laid out (apparently, your personal bed), a limited number of cute little dresses hung directly on nails on one of the walls, plus the pair of shoes that I brought and put carefully beside another pair in order not to spoil the harmony of the ensemble . . ."

"And Motheh?" Mrs. Gerda asked with interest (she stared into the void, above my head).

"'My Savior!' she shouted, 'you are my Savior . . . !' She had come to. I ask you to note that she undressed herself a little in her death throes. That I could have ignored but not this 'Savior' thing. I felt like throwing up . . . I looked at her, her face looked like it was carved in lime and her hair looked like silver, I couldn't tear my eyes away from it. She had lice too . . ."

"She did," admitted Mrs. Gerda, "how could she avoid it? She was ill, she couldn't comb heh haih anymohe . . ."

Her voice quavered slightly, between embarrassment and tenderness. It seemed to me that I had hurt her feelings.

"You are a cultivated woman," I continued, "and it's impossible not to know that even in ancient Greece there were similar cases. A number of philosophers, otherwise clean enough, perished from the illness called 'lice.' Lice walked on them, like words. It seems that even Plato . . ."

"It's possible," sighed Mrs. Gerda, "but in ouh family—"

"It doesn't matter," I said. "Every country and every family has its own lice . . ."

*Methusaleh, the oldest goldfish in Europe, passed away in Berlin at the age of 55.

21. I was beginning to feel sorry for having hurt her feelings.

"Maybe I did wrong, Mrs. Gerda," I said, "but why do

you force me to evoke? You know very well that I can't stand this . . ."

"It's all hight," she answered. "I don't eveh get mad at you because you ahe like a child." (It seemed that she had understood me, but the wrong way round.) "We can stop evoking if you want to—"

"No, no," I objected. "Even if we say different things, we talk about the same thing. Let's evoke, Mrs. Gerda!" (A trace of enthusiasm had crept into my voice.) "Why not evoke?" And I continued: "You know, I stood at the old woman's head and wondered how on earth she was able to throw those shoes with such precision when she could hardly move . . . That's what puzzles me even now . . ."

"Sometimes Motheh had powehs," explained Mrs. Gerda. (She looked reconciled now.) "She dhessed me, she said I was helpless. Without moving, she used to send the dhess, oh the shiht, oh the dhessing gown sailing though the aih, they came by themselves . . ."

"Oh, Mrs. Gerda," I said, "You are amazing, believe me! How can you say such a thing . . . ?"

"Then let's dhop it," she proposed (she smiled, I had to become cautious again). "Tell me, how is evehything going . . . ?"

"Thanks," I replied. "Look, a few moments ago I played a game where we all lived in a vast cemetery and we called to each other, each from his own coffin . . ."

"My ghave is still neah youhs, isn't it?" sighed Mrs. Gerda. Her eyes were misty, she again had that slight quaver in her voice.

Then she withdrew her bust from the other side of the window, back inside the pharmacy.

"I should be going," she said, "I have a date with my husband, I see him coming . . ."

I turned my head and looked down the street. Only a few moments later, a little old man in a frock coat appeared from around the corner of Domniței Boulevard, he walked slowly leaning on a stick with a silver knob, he tried to hold himself erect.

"Mrs. Gerda," I said, "I know your husband, I've met him, but I wasn't even aware of the relationship . . ."

"We all know each otheh, but we fohget the helationship," she reminded me. Then she exchanged a few words with the pharmacist, who didn't budge from his white chair, and went toward the door.

Once outside, when she was close, I stopped her.

"Excuse me," I said, "but I must ask you something before we part: now, in your present life, do you use the same chamber pot?"

Mrs. Gerda smiled. "I have a new one, with little flowehs," she answered, "a wedding phesent fhom my husband . . ."

Then she went away as if floating in the yellow semidarkness of the streetlights. When she got to her husband, he kissed her hand gallantly. They quickly disappeared, arm in arm, around the first corner.

It was our last encounter, and I don't exactly know whether all three of us were present.

VII

■ □ ■ □ ■

THE PLANK

I. THE SIGNS, WHICH I MIGHT HAVE INSISTED ON TOO MUCH, entitled me to foresee the approaching of a kind of beginning and end, toward which I seemed to be heading. Except for moments of weakness, still frequent enough, I waited calmly for something that might or might not come (it was all the same to me). Chasing away the explanatory temptations, my active side, although decisive, had only to maintain me in a state of receptiveness.

Thus, it so happened that on a Friday, wandering the streets at random, I reached the outer limits of the city. I sensed the proximity of the field. I walked along a wretched street with its ditches invaded by weeds. The houses looked unnaturally small, mere huts. Four children crouched on the concrete stairs of a more presentable building, apparently a butcher shop. After a while I stopped. That was the place I was looking for, an immense yard surrounded by a rotten old wood fence, with planks yellowed by rain and sun thrown haphazardly in there. Above the gate, an almost erased sign: LUMBER YARD.

I opened the gate and went in. I had the feeling that I knew that yard well, as if from a dream. Toward the back of the yard was a dilapidated house with a single room on the second floor, and among the planks moved the familiar figure of a short and tired little old man, I approached him.

"Good morning, Mr. Sima," I said.

The old man turned and looked at me for a moment.

"You can call me whatever you like," he replied, "but you're confusing me with somebody else . . ."

Maybe it wasn't exactly him, maybe I was mistaken, but they resembled each other too much, so I decided to continue calling him that.

Mr. Sima sat down on a plank, he had a very small mouth, and he smiled with it; I felt offended: I was glad to see him again, but why did he trick me back then with his frozen tears?

"Last winter you were crying, Mr. Sima, you said you were dying, you tried to persuade me—"

"Wait a second," he said, "you're obviously confusing me with someone else . . ."

"Let's drop it, Mr. Sima," I said, "you might be capable of crying even now, like that driver who gave me a free tour of Bucharest and cried as he showed me all the cultural institutions of the city, including the Education Building . . ."

"He might have been drunk," Mr. Sima said calmly, while I waited for the deep boredom, the void, and the lack of confidence that follow after too strong a solicitation.

Little by little the distant rumble of the city fell silent, as if melted by the heat (I thought of Zenobia, as the witness and judge of my existence), I felt like sitting down on the plank beside that little man.

"What can we do, Mr. Sima?" I asked. "Sometimes we think that we are the hub of the universe, and maybe we are, because this universe has a lot of hubs . . ."

I stopped to breathe, Mr. Sima was looking off to the side, I sat down beside him on the plank.

---

*In Corsica, a man obsessed with traffic rules was put in jail. From the window of his house he had fired his rifle at the drivers who didn't observe the rules of the roundabout.

2. We sat for a while on that plank, the sun was still rather hot, Mr. Sima was silent, he smiled with his little mouth, I could have slapped that mouth, then I forgot about him. I felt that the moment was approaching when all my movements during those last days were going to make their own connections.

From time to time the requital, now impotent and sporadic, tempted me. ("Not one of the millions of people who have populated this poor earth from time immemorial preserved for us the image of miraculous love, and all believed that they did love. No one knows how brilliant love is anymore," and so on . . .)

This lasted for one moment and then another. Up in the sky a little white cloud had appeared, it bore the exact outline of my face. Where my left ear should have been, another little cloud, somewhat smaller, attached itself, it looked through me. Then they melted together, they flowed through one another like fraternal waters ("Don't leave me alone, Zenobia!"), I was inside myself, alone, even though loneliness had disappeared. Nothing could have undone our embrace. An immense silence, as between two thunderclaps, had grown around us. I saw beyond, where heavenly bodies spun, and beyond them. We floated, light and free, above the earth where our bodies filled with a sense of uselessness and the void waited for us, distances seemed, I don't know how to put it, nostalgic. The ocean of silence rumbled with the noise of the rotation inside us, the axes of the world thundered between the pillars of our embrace, "I'm glad you came," said Mr. Sima, "maybe we're seeing each other for the first time . . ."

I was again beside him on the plank in that yard invaded by weeds.

*Charles Smith, 137, had his second leg amputated. His first leg had been amputated two years before because of circulatory problems.

3. Then I heard again the rumble of the city, apparently in the streets the quick and the dead had resumed the usual bustling off to their precise business.

Mr. Sima stared into the void, he looked like a wretch, like a dead dog, I think he was fatigued by the cruel scorching of the sun. He broke chips off the plank under us.

"Rotten wood," he said, "the corpse of a corpse . . ."

I felt ashamed, but let's drop it . . . (I had learned on my own to think with my hands.)

"Maybe it's time to review," I said. "From one person's mouth to another person's ear, a pair of scales is born, like it or not . . ."

Mr. Sima looked up for an instant and shed some tears because of the too bright light.

"Now," he sighed, "I'm too old to review, hairs have grown inside my ears, you can see them with your naked eye . . ."

Then he leaned toward me. "Look into my ear," he said.

I looked into his ear, I could see nothing but that yellowish tip and the gluey black hole covered by white and curly little hairs.

"Maybe deeper inside," he said, "where the darkness begins." But even there I could see nothing.

"What do you see?" asked Mr. Sima.

"Nothing," I replied.

"Too bad!" he tried to comfort me. "It would be nice to be able to see each other's thoughts . . . That means you came all this way for nothing . . ."

"In any case, you're not at all to blame," I said. "I still consider you a wise man, even though your wisdom, like your ear, seems rather smelly to me . . . But let's imagine that I have come to ask you the question . . ."

"What question?"

He seemed amused and frightened at the same time. He had raised his eyebrows and frowned, you would have thought that he was about to burst out laughing or run away.

"Don't worry, Mr. Sima," I reassured him, "I won't ask

the question you have in mind. Maybe I don't even know it . . . This time I'll ask you something simple, something that can be said . . ."

"Then go ahead, ask me, you can do it, nobody can stop you, right? Look, why don't you ask me about the Kalahari Desert, for example, or whatever you like, but take into account that I know nothing—what could I possibly know? And even if I ever knew anything, you can be sure that I've forgotten it."

"It doesn't matter, Mr. Sima," I said, "you're old, that's your business, but maybe you know one of the old men's truths that I couldn't possibly know, or some other truth . . ."

"Look," said Mr. Sima (and you would have thought that he was talking to himself, in his own ear), "I remember only one of the truths, as you call them, which you couldn't possibly know because you haven't been there. It is the only one that I can communicate to you and I ask you to remember it: when you are very old, or even sometime sooner, you piss in your pants. This is the only truth that I still remember . . ."

"You, Mr. Sima," I said, "are playing a game with me, one that I never liked . . ."

"Too bad," said Mr. Sima, and he smiled, I again felt like slapping him. "It was a beautiful game, I remember we enjoyed playing it sometimes. But maybe it would be better if we went indoors, the sun is too hot, though it's long past noon . . ."

"Let's go, Mr. Sima, why not?" I agreed, and we both got up from the plank and went indoors, to the upstairs room.

*A team of Australian zoologists discovered a species of frog that differs from all others in that it is capable of hatching its eggs in its own stomach and then giving birth to its fully developed young through its mouth.

4. It was cooler inside the house, anyway, the sun didn't burn our heads anymore, but because the light outside was so strong,

we could hardly see, we had to grope our way up the stairs.

"Do you want me to fix you some tea?" asked Mr. Sima from somewhere near me, I could more feel than hear him.

"No, Mr. Sima," I said, "I don't want you to."

"Very well," agreed Mr. Sima, "then let's sit down," and I felt him push a chair toward me but I didn't sit down.

After a while, my eyes grew accustomed to the dim light. The only window of the room was covered by a rather crooked black paper curtain, under it there was a long and narrow wooden table, on which lay a human shape, a kind of mannequin, I went closer to that shape, I removed the paper curtain, light filled the room.

"Lo and behold," I said, "it's none other than Mrs. Gerda's husband, the whipped-cream-eater . . ."

And I shook him pretty hard, "Wake up," I said, "and go get some ice cream for the three of us . . ."

He didn't budge, he seemed not to hear me, he was sound asleep in his impeccable frock coat, he held in his left hand the cane with the silver head.

"A waste of time," said Mr. Sima, "he won't wake up for three days . . ."

"Then let's not disturb his sleep," I said, and I was wondering why I was talking in whispers. "So, Mr. Sima, you live together . . ."

"Not at all!" explained Mr. Sima. "He is only passing through, to gain more consistency . . ."

"If he's sleeping," I said aloud this time, "maybe it would be better to be quiet."

"You're right," agreed Mr. Sima. "Let's sit down and be quiet."

We sat down, each in his chair, and were quiet for a long while.

*Two blind Englishmen succeeded in crossing the English Channel on water skis.

ZENOBIA

172

5. Because I was bored watching over the sleeping man, I started to look out the window. From the upstairs room I could see only the treetops, an acacia to the left, a giant walnut with two main branches in front and to the left, and a string of poplars on the horizon.

After a while the treetops imperceptibly started moving to and fro, each one differently, the top of the acacia trembled slightly, I could only guess at the swaying of the poplars, the sky seemed to be stuck to them, it moved in time with them in a kind of compact motion, the tops of the walnut tree rose indifferently, as in wintertime when trees forget the sap deep in their trunks.

I was thinking of the plank outside, on which I had sat, maybe it vibrated too. An impetuous sap invaded the world, its thrill touched the uppermost branch of the walnut tree, turned toward the acacia . . . In the free part of the sky a bird stopped, I knew it was dead, that was me on the dreadful green catafalque, I hovered in the air, round and motionless, with folded wings.

A few leaves stretched out to caress me, the poplars came closer and with them the acacia. They stuck to me, covering me. It was getting dark, but I could make out in detail every little branch, every leaf, every vein, I even saw the reddish-yellow spots on the few leaves of the walnut tree that had forgotten to fall off in winter.

I floated in that halo, the treetops had covered the whole horizon, I felt good there, I watched myself with tenderness and with no trace of regret. A liquid, bittersweet melancholy flowed through me . . .

Suddenly everything retreated, I reentered myself, I sat on the chair in front of the window, that man continued to sleep quietly face up, while next to him Mr. Sima sat on his chair and drew with his right index finger an invisible and continuous circle above his right knee.

Later, when I left, I felt a strong need to urinate.

THE PLANK

*The Swiss fakir, Mirna Bey (under his real name, Augustin Fournier), went down the 10,000-foot-high Saas Fee glacier stretched out on sharp nails driven through a plank. Mirna Bey, who was wearing only a leopard-skin bikini and a turban on his head, used the bed of nails as a sled.

6. The coming of fall had covered the sky with transparent glass. Everything seemed shiny. I was on the street, near Philanthropy Square, I was reading an ad written in ink on a flyer pasted to a pole. Someone had lost his dog and was offering a good reward for finding him. Maria passed by on the other side of the street, she walked as if in a trance, she didn't see me.

I crossed the street, I caught up with her, she stopped. Her eyes shone, perhaps because of the sky, but she shivered in her wrinkled dress. One of her stockings was white, the other blue.

"Maria," I said, "where have you been all this time? Your parents are desperately looking for you . . ."

"I'm going home," she replied.

She had a flat voice that didn't seem to participate in the meaning of her words. A sad resignation covered her face. Perhaps they who at the dawn of Marathon waited for their deaths looked like that. Except they prepared to meet death by gracefully combing their long hair . . .

"That's good," I said, "because filial love does exist, I know one case—that of Pero, the daughter of Cimon, who was sentenced to death by starvation by his fellow citizens, but she saved him by breast-feeding him daily with her incestuous milk . . ."

I expected my rather stupid joke to bring Maria back to where we were, but she seemed not to hear me, she stood before me like a desert plain.

"I'm going home," she repeated. "I'm going to get married . . ."

Words came out of her mouth like knives she threw at

herself but they scratched me too in their mad trajectory. The requital whispered to me that it wasn't I who had decided on this meeting. I thought of not thinking anymore, but I would have liked to pull Maria out of her slough of despond.

"Let me tell you something" (I was talking fast, one might even have thought that I was jovial), "about two years ago I invented a game, I called it 'the horizontal': I would put several lives in a line, I didn't need too many of them, and I would find myself, for instance, near Raymondus Lullus, I spoke with him in Catalan. After a while the game bored me, it had too much plague and cholera in it. Then I decided to change it, to go vertical, and I let my beard grow. When it had grown long enough, I shaved my left cheek together with the respective side of the mustache . . ."

Maria was silent, she stared sadly into the void, she seemed to be a child-woman, but her soul stunk of dead dog.

"Listen, I had big plans," I continued. "With only half a beard I prepared for my hot date. Do you remember? I came to you too, in the studio . . . After that I shaved the remaining half of my beard and moved into a corridor on Moşilor Way at Domniţei Boulevard. After that I left for the swamps—"

"It's Assistant Lecturer Ioachim that I'm marrying," Maria interrupted. "Mother will burst with joy . . ."

"And Jason?" I asked her.

"I don't know anymore. I hope he croaked too . . ."

She spoke very reluctantly, she could hardly bear her words. I had the vertiginous sensation of someone who enters a room where he knows the exact place of each little thing and, look, he finds everything upside down, destroyed, covered by debris.

"Wait," I said, "I know another case with a likable boy, one Robescu. This one always said 'après vous,' he liked it. If you were with him and wanted to enter a room, he would politely step aside and say *'après vous'* and let you in first. If he wanted to smoke, he would take out the pack of cigarettes, offer you one, say *'après vous,'* and so on. I think that he came into this world only to say *'après vous'* and trick us because he croaked before all of us: he was the first to die, when he was nineteen . . ."

I listened to my rant. I saw the whole muddle of the ball of thread that I had believed well organized. I knew the thread, I could have grabbed an end and pulled, but it couldn't be done like that, so suddenly. I was afraid of adding to the muddle.

"They suffocated me," said Maria. "They have suffocated me ever since I was a child . . ."

But apparently she guessed my anxiety, she thought of sparing me.

"This time we were born all wrong, but it's all right," she sighed. "Maybe next time . . ."

Then she leaned toward me, I was wearing a pin with a snake. "It's beautiful," she said. "Can you let me wear it, just for a little while?"

"You can have it" (I was glad, it seemed to me that she was recovering). "I have another one in my pocket, with a pair of scales. I found them on the street . . ."

She took the pin and fastened it to her dress. "I'll keep it as a souvenir," she said.

She had puffed out her frail chest, she was caressing the pin. I looked at her: feeble as she was she had to carry on an ancient and terrible battle.

Then I inverted the question that one usually asks children: "Whom do you hate the most? Your mother or your father?"

"Both, by turns," she replied, without hesitation. "Both of them, but my mother more . . ."

Then we fell silent for a moment, before parting. Maria was smiling as if she were from another world, she was caressing the pin.

*A baby born to a gorilla at the Columbus Zoo was taken away from his mother because she didn't want to feed him and held him upside down all the time.

7. A few days later, I told Zenobia that it was about time to return to the swamps. "We're done here, we have things to do over there . . ."

I was certain that Zenobia understood exactly what I wanted to say even though I was silent.

"And when do you think we should go?" she asked.

"Maybe as soon as tomorrow . . ."

I was smiling. I remembered how once, a while ago, in March, I stood in the corridor of a third-class train car, it was very crowded, I couldn't move my arms. I had come early to that commuter station, we still had a quarter of an hour until departure, when the door of a packed compartment flew open. On the threshold appeared a tall, skinny young man, who was terribly pale. He was accompanied by a short woman, she barely came up to the middle of his chest, she held his hand like one holds a blind man or a child.

"Pardon-noose!" she shouted (she wanted to express herself as beautifully as possible), "Pardon-noose . . . !"

The others did their best to let them through. If one of the passengers wouldn't let them by, the short woman would beg him, pointing up at the man's tortured face: "He's sick . . . He ate a whole bucket of mucenici* . . ."

This convincing argument helped her to take her husband down the corridor and get him off between the tracks.

Once there, the man squatted weakly right in front of the windows of my car and pulled down his pants . . . He had a sad, confused look. The woman stood next to him and repeated desperately: "Pardon-noose . . . ! Pardon-noose . . . !"

The others showed such an understanding toward their

*A dish eaten at Lent; the literal meaning is "martyrs."—TRANS.

fellow man that I was touched, like at the movies when the innocent hero dies in his lover's arms. They pretended not to see him, they looked above him, toward other tracks with freight cars . . .

*As part of the research on Parkinson's disease, studies were initiated in a field unknown until now—that of biochemical regulators of human instincts and emotions.

8. So the next day we left the city. The train was leaving from the same commuter station. This time, maybe because it was noon, there were enough free seats, but we stood by the window to look at fields of corn turned yellow, at the muddy waters of the Sabar River, at the bluish meadows of the Argeș and Neajlov Rivers lost among ghostlike swamps and dark forests . . .

When we got off at that station, waves of serene quiet flooded from the top of my head to the soles of my feet and drained into the ground. They made me dizzy, it was good. The train went on toward the Danube, for a moment I imagined it plunging into the waters of the river like a clumsy hippopotamus, its skin scorched by the sun. We crossed the empty bridge. Beyond it, in the distance, stood the dam and the edge of the still-green reeds of the swamp.

I walked for a while with Zenobia, the beginning of fall had covered the wild bareness of the place with mauve-and-rust-colored flowers. On the dam the dirt was black and cracked, we could have imagined ourselves on the crater of a volcano.

When the railroad station was well behind us and when in front of us to the right of the swamps appeared the red spot of the forest, I told Zenobia:

"I'll leave you here. Maybe I'll be late. Now go and wait for me . . ."

"I'll wait," said Zenobia, and she kissed me on the cheek.

For a while I followed her thin and lonely figure along the dam. She stopped a few times and waved to me.

"Behave yourself," she shouted.

*Over 350,000 Canadians participated in the popular running, bicycling, and running-on-stilts competitions in the first annual sports festival organized in memory of Terry Fox, a young man who became famous for having started the Marathon of Hope while suffering from cancer and having his leg amputated.

Among others in the competition were a blind girl from Ottawa and a 73-year-old woman from Thunder Bay, Ontario.

9. I climbed down from the dam toward the plain through heaps of weeds and wildflowers, I spoke to them. Maybe because of my still-urban appearance, they tripped me and threw me to the ground. A few times they scratched my hands and face.

A blue bird asked for something, I took a piece of bread from my pocket and offered it on my open palm. The bird scooped it up on the fly. It could have taken my eyes as well.

I walked in random zigzags, I went round in circles, I knew that no matter how long I wandered I would arrive on time. Uphill, on the edge of the forest, a road appeared, I knew it, I didn't trust it at all.

Then the sheep flooded in, whole flocks of them. As far as I could see, it seemed to me that the dust of the earth shook, throbbed, and bleated. A trembling avalanche slid by on thousands of little feet.

The flocks were not herded by dogs, they were driven by the shouts of some soldier-shepherds, naked to their waists and darkened by the sun. Wearing rough, yellowish cloth trousers, dragging with difficulty their dusty army boots, the soldier-shepherds walked, shouting and whirling their staffs in the air like giant wands. Each one of them made different sounds, peculiar to himself, the strangest sounds I have ever heard. I felt, however, a kind of shyness in them: it was obvious that the sheep weren't theirs but belonged to the merciless and invisible Great Master, from whom nothing could escape. The soldier-shepherds, likewise driven here through the hostile heat of the plain, walked as if in a trance, their foreheads to the sky, whistling, shouting, yelling, moaning, meowing, groaning, barking. They walked, hallucinating, with their eyes turned upward, imitating the birds, the wind, and the leaves. They didn't care about anything but the sheep that they addressed with an amazing cowardice. I heard one of them trying to flatter a hulk of a ram who had rested his muzzle on the ground, a few steps from me.

"Come on, *stag* . . . !" he said.

Then above the uproar I heard a distant voice: "Hey, the cows . . . ! Watch out or they'll kill 'em . . . !"

Then the soldier-shepherds started to utter other sounds, other shouts, other yells, equally amazing. And the sheep, which understood them perfectly, rushed to the sides of the meadow, clearing the way.

The herd of cows came slowly down the road from the forest, with their moist eyes and dreadful horns.

*On finding out that sheep suffer more from the damp than from the cold, a sheep breeder from New Zealand, and after him other sheep breeders from Great Britain, made the sheep wear waterproof polyethylene clothes.

10. I stayed there for a while, I felt good in the soft cobweb of the meadow, I would have stayed longer, but the sky had imperceptibly turned violet and over the line of the hill appeared an ugly cloud, as if made of tar, and I thought I should look for shelter.

I knew some old willow trees nearby, they were hollow and dirty, some time ago I had caressed the long, muddy threads hanging on their trunks like long hair, and I set off toward them.

I walked hurriedly because the sky was rapidly darkening and I heard the distant, muffled echo of thunder. Then lightning bolts suddenly started to fall around me.

They came in bursts, one after the other, as if from a gigantic, perfectly zeroed-in machine-gun, they fell crackling and rumbling, their light blinded me, they fell in an exact circle with a constant diameter, circling me and following me step by step, as if playing a demented game. I was at the center of the circle that advanced with me and stopped precisely whenever I stumbled.

When I reached the willow trees, I rushed to one of them and crouched there, between the branches. The fire grew more intense, still keeping me at its center.

I sat down with my forehead against the trunk, the branches stung me, ants started walking on my face, through my eyelids I saw the red-and-black explosions, I vibrated to the rumble of the sky, it seemed to me that the end had come and I waited, I don't know why, for the flood of devastating waters.

Naturally, I wasn't afraid: catastrophic grandeur excludes minor panic. I stayed there, under the lightning bolts, in an end that wasn't mine, I could die, it didn't depend only on me, I had entered into the grandeur of other laws, and they didn't make me impotent. I was the way I was, I sat the way I sat, but what I felt wasn't at all like death. I remembered well: once, when I had died for a little while, I was flooded by a boundless melancholy, pleasant and serene. Back then I was sinking into a sort of tender and resigned kindness, I floated in the zones of an immense regret, painless but mournful. Now—nothing like that: I sat there like a rock, a branch, or a wild animal with the feelings of a rock, a branch, or a wild animal, participating completely and actively. I was a small part of the void, ready to reenter the matrix without being lost, in a natural way and without a trace of sadness.

Shortly after, perhaps (I don't know anymore), the lightning-bolt circle abandoned me. The rumble resounded farther and farther away, behind the hill. Then it fell silent, and a terrible quiet ensued.

*Every fall, on rainy moonless nights, in the Indian village of Jatinga (Assam), huge flocks of birds of different species gather. They fly toward any source of light, no matter how strong, crashing on the ground or flying in circles at great speed for a long time, until they drop exhausted. Interestingly, they are attracted only by light sources no more than half a mile from the center of the village.

11. I stopped on a hill just below a vineyard and a dry cornfield. At my feet, under the steep slope, the river flowed lazily. I stretched out on the ground, I knew each and every boulder, each and every tree. Lower, in the middle of the water, was the precise limit of my last wanderings in that worn-out boat (I seemed to feel in my soles the rotten wood under the layer of tar). There, on a little island, I used to meet a white goat with a strangely long beard, she had red eyes, she would come to the bank to greet me, I would ask "How are you, miss?" and sometimes she answered me by bleating in her own language.

Now the island was deserted, its weeds had turned yellow, while over here, along the slope, the still-green weeds moved in the wind.

I looked at the landscape: only the boat, the satisfied fisherman, and some ducklings, possibly wild, plus the swan and the hunter with his faithful dog and the mill, were lacking for me to feel as if in a little poem by my personal enemy, Johann Wolfgang von Goethe (*wurde im Jahre siebzehnhundertneunundvierzig zu Frankfurt am Main geboren. Seine Eltern waren . . .* and so on).

Then I was approached by an ugly man wearing a shirt blackened with dirt, which was slit from the waist almost up to the back of his neck, and rubber shoes. The man dragged a little metal cart crammed with herbs and weeds. He pulled it with difficulty, panting, he walked diagonally across the slope, I feared he might fall.

Having arrived in front of me, the man stopped and greeted me, he blocked the wheels of the cart with two dry clods and sat down to smoke a cigarette.

"Seems to me that I know you from somewhere," he began after inhaling once or twice.

"I don't think so," I replied.

"Didn't I bring you milk in the summertime?" he resumed.

"Certainly not," I assured him.

"Then my wife brought it, that's it," he persisted.

"Absolutely not . . ."

"Too bad," said the man. "We had goat's milk, which is the best because it even cures consumption . . ."

"And now you don't have any more?" I asked offhandedly.

"No, I don't," he replied.

I looked toward the island. The white goat had appeared, I don't know where from. Even though she was rather far away, I could see her laughing at me and shaking her little beard.

"Why don't you have milk anymore?" I asked that Goethe. "Your goat died?"

"What do you mean?" (The man looked at me suspiciously.) "In the summertime we had four, counting the old one, but I had to give away one of the kids because my wife played with them too much, she didn't have time for anything else, because they play, you know . . . Truth to tell, it's easier for me with only three of them instead of four when I take them to graze, because they won't eat just anything, anywhere. You take them out on a chain, and they pull you here and there, they choose food by the taste, after that they play, they like that . . . When I stopped to catch my breath, the little ones played with me, they trampled me under their feet, they trampled me right here, and on my head . . ."

I was looking toward the island. The white goat had vanished like smoke. I thought it wasn't possible, she didn't have anywhere to hide in the short weeds . . .

"And you follow them like this all the time?" I asked, to keep the conversation going.

"Why shouldn't I? I get three barrels of cheese from them, and I get milk, eggs too, everything, I have everything I need, let the winter come, I don't care . . ."

"The eggs come from them too?"

"What do you mean, 'from them'?" (The man looked again at me with surprise and suspicion.) "The eggs are from the hens, everybody knows that, but from the goats I get cheese and milk, I have everything . . . That's why I gather weeds for them, because they eat a lot of them. They like them . . ." He seemed delighted. "In the summer I gathered a whole stack. I'll finish a second one by the time they get home . . ."

"But where are they?"

"With the billy goat, where did you think? I took them to the billy goat, in another township, because there they have clear spring water too, I keep them there as long as necessary. For the old one I pay 180 lei in cash, that man milks her but now he's not getting much, about a quart a day, that's still something . . . For the little ones I pay another 100 each . . ."

"And the billy goat," I feigned some interest, "is he doing a good job?"

"He is," he replied. "The little ones are from him . . ."

"I also knew a goat around here, a white one" (I pointed to the island). "Is it yours?"

"How could that be?" He seemed offended. "That's another one who was killed by a hard life. It was Chitic's, that poor old devil . . . He wanted to get a kid from me, from the seed of the old one, instead of her, but I didn't give her to him, why would I? He kept begging me, he said that he would pay as much as I wanted, but I told him: 'Hey, you're wasting your time because I won't give her to you to torture on the island tied to a peg like a martyr. No matter how much money you offer, I'm not giving her to you because I'll slaughter her in the fall, I'll make pastrami out of her and eat it with my wife . . .'"

"And when did all this happen?"

"Last summer," he said, "about two months ago, when the white one died. But, just so you know, she still appears to some people and laments her fate . . . It's worse when she appears as a hawk, with feathers, because she can peck your head until blood flows, you have no idea what she's capable of doing . . ."

"There she is!" I said (she laughed at me from the island).

The man looked, then turned to me.

"I don't see her, she appears only to you. If she's feather-less, that's good. That means it's time to go you-know-where . . ."

With that, the man slowly got up, dropped the cigarette butt that had gone out long ago between his thin blue-violet lips, squashed it carefully with the sole of his rubber shoe, bid farewell, and left, dragging his cart through his goatish universe.

Intuiting somehow the exemplary meaning of his existence, I turned once more toward the deserted island. Then I set off too, dragged by the chain of my goats along the edge of the swamp toward Mr. Sima's house, which was now covered in rust-colored ivy.

*At the Cultural Center of Tenggarong, near Samarinda (on the eastern coast of Borneo), there is a strange animal, a mixture of tiger, bird, goat, and elephant, that was captured in the Borneo jungle. The animal has the hooves of a goat, the claws of a bird, the body of a tiger, wings, the trunk of an elephant, and horns, and stands about three feet tall.

12. When I got there, I knocked at the gate, I knew that no one would answer. Then I jumped over the fence. Dry leaves

rustled under my steps, the walnuts had turned black, they fell to the ground, I stepped over them too.

The door was ajar, but I didn't go in. I stepped onto the veranda at the front of the house, I sat down on a flimsy bench near a little table. I saw fresh signs of habitation around me, as if the house had been abandoned in a great hurry not long before.

The veranda, a few square yards in size and sunken in a deserted silence, had two sides enclosed by windows and two open sides.

I sat on the bench and thought of various things, machines of the time. I held in my hand a playing card that I had found under the bench, the jack of clubs, naturally.

I thought, for instance, of the mad scissors that one day bit my fingers when I wanted to cut my nails, of the belt buckle that bruised me every morning when I freed the dust from my trousers, of that cursed razor blade that scratched my chin every time I wanted to shave, of the little plum tree twig that tried to pierce my eyes one evening, of the hammer that hit me out of rancor and blackened one of my fingernails just because I was passing by, and so on . . .

Of course, such things can happen to anyone and they are easily forgotten. But when five times a day you hurt yourself on the same rock that you move aside each time, and when your toe is bruised and hurts so much that it makes you howl, you become cautious, like it or not, you start to think that the rock lay there in wait only for you to come by . . .

Then I put the jack of clubs on the table and thought of nothing.

*In Dalton (Massachusetts) tens of thousands of caterpillars took over the trees of a neighborhood, eventually entering the homes too. Several apartments were evacuated. Strong water jets, giant vacuum cleaners, etc., were used against the invaders. It is hoped that soon all the leaves of the trees will be devoured by the caterpillars, causing the death of those unwanted visitors.

13. Then came the bumblebee. Flying about in his gorgeous yellow and brown stripes, he dashed buzzing into the west window of the veranda. He struggled desperately to get through it to the other side. He clung with his legs, he flew round in circles, he fell . . . Beyond the windowpane, on the apparently clear horizon, the sun was floating deep in an orange light. The bumblebee wanted to get there at any price. And he bumped so hard against the glass that I felt sorry for him.

"Hey, bumblebee," I said, "don't you see that there is a window in front of you and because of it the path that you think is clear is only an illusion? Because you can see through it, you can't see. The simplicity of the error stops you and knocks you to the ground. That's what's happening to both of us: we struggle blinded by transparencies. Why don't you try more to the right or more to the left, where you think there's nothing . . ."

But he struggled furiously, he stubbornly defended his fierce trajectory, he struck the window with his wings and little feet, he tried to break it, he persisted in trying to get through to the other side.

When he fell dizzy for the nth time, I wanted to help him, to pick him up on the playing card as if it were a dustpan and throw him out one of the clear sides. But I looked for him in vain. He had disappeared. He had found the way by himself . . .

I remained on the bench, I don't know for how long. The time of errors had passed. The sun began to set. Dogs were barking in the distance. Two people were walking through a dense tree. Maybe they had some scaffolding there, maybe they were building a tower—who knows?—but from the veranda I could see only them and the tree. Them walking through a tree.

THE PLANK

Once they had climbed down, the time had come for me to enter the house too . . .

*Claude Pepper notes that there are at least 500,000 known cases of violence against elderly people committed by the victims' own children or grandchildren.

14. I knocked at the door, nobody answered. I went in.

In the downstairs room it was so quiet I could hear my own breathing. The sweetish aroma of Mr. Sima's long-wilted flowers hung in the air. The dust of abandonment had settled all over the place, that rifle was still in its place, hanging on the wall, I thought for a moment of taking it but I dropped the idea, I didn't need the rifle.

I went upstairs. Light and dark didn't exist anymore, I mean to say that everything was happening in a strange twilight, I mean to say that light and dark had melted into each other in an incomprehensible and indescribable radiance.

In the upstairs room I noticed Dragoş (I saw him through my closed eyelids), he was sleeping facing the door, crouching on a blue table under the window that overlooked the swamps.

He looked unchanged, he wore the same ancient rags. Except on his feet, instead of peasant shoes, he wore a pair of sneakers.

I went closer to him.

"Wake up," I said, "let's have a talk."

He didn't budge, he remained obstinately asleep. Beyond the window the tops of the reeds swayed in the wind, random birds flew here and there just above them. I counted them attentively, there were nine.

I pulled a chair up to the table and sat down with the palms of my hands resting on my knees, as if at a wake.

"Dra-a-agoş," I said (I spoke, I don't know why, with a drawl; a kind of sad and muffled lamentation was coming out of my mouth), "where did you leave the chi-i-ild? Did you give him up for adoptio-o-on?"

He didn't answer, but I was sure that he heard me.

"Do you feel like playing to-o-o?" I continued. "Or maybe you're not interested and you want to chat about something e-e-else . . ."

Then I rested my forehead against the edge of the blue table, the paint was still fresh, it stuck to my hair, my eyes itched even though I kept them closed.

"Why don't you answer me?" I asked. "You know very well that I'm a chi-i-ild, maybe that very chi-i-ild. Do you want me to stretch my a-a-rm to wipe off the dust that's fallen on your mou-u-uth . . .?"

I stood up and pushed the chair aside.

"Hey, Dragoş," I said (no longer lamenting, I had regained my normal voice), "somewhere, I don't remember where, there is a giant whale, she swims in seas and oceans, maybe she's the one who decides . . . Stuck to her belly is the male, as tiny as a match. He stays there motionless, as you do now, and functions only when she feels the need to get pregnant. Afterward he resumes his motionlessness. And you, Dragoş, you're silent and pretend to sleep, but to no avail. I look at you, you're exactly like that male, except you're incredibly old. Maybe you sleep stuck to her unseen belly or inside the belly, who knows . . . ?"

Dragoş was silent, the light stung my eyes, it made me dizzy. I took a few steps across the room, then I came back next to him.

"Hey, you asshole," I said, to balance myself, "where did you get those stinking sneakers from? You think you're a sportsman now . . . ?"

I was talking alone, painfully alone. I saw and heard myself, and felt like crying. It was extremely difficult, maybe once again I hadn't sufficiently prepared. The lucid impulse of requital stirred up all the yeast of my vanity mixed with the doubt and distrust of myself.

THE PLANK

"I must inform you, friend," I said (I spoke loudly, I almost yelled), "that a while ago I played sports too and, listen, I tackled beautifully, I was fast too, I was all will and force, I didn't think of anything, it was sheer madness . . . ! I pushed in the scrummage with my shoulders and the back of my neck, desperate and happy. Sometimes I found myself out of the scrummage with the ball in my arms and I ran as if this was the sole aim of my existence, as if once I had reached the goal line, one of the great wonders of the world would happen. Then everything around me disappeared, it seemed to me that I had been running for centuries on an endless field. The others ran like mad to catch me from behind and knock me down. I could have passed the ball and then another one would have become the target of their fury, but I kept on running . . ."

I heard my voice, I was ashamed of myself.

"And I must inform you, friend, that once, while I was running like this, an elderly man appeared in front of me whom I knew very well because I had seen him in a café where he sat at a table with a child, the two of them eating ice cream (when he left he threw a coin at me; then I saw him arm in arm with Mrs. Gerda, but you don't know Mrs. Gerda, she exists, a friend of mine . . .). Moreover, I had met him at Mr. Sima's place, in the storage room, he pretended to be asleep, just like you . . . Then on the field, that man gestured for me to stop, he asked: 'Why are you running? Where are you running to?' 'You, sir,' I replied, 'haven't the slightest idea, and if I told you, you wouldn't even believe me . . .' Actually, I didn't quite know myself either, but it was all the same to me, it didn't interest me . . ."

Dragoș remained silent. The light penetrated my skin, it tried to petrify me. I thought for a second of Zenobia, I saw her as if she were a few steps away from me: she sat quietly, her hands in her lap, at the entrance of our hollow, on a heap of dry reeds. She was waiting for me. "Help me!" I shouted to her.

"You pretend to be dead and you're quiet," I said then to Dragoş, "you forget that you're a child too . . ."

Then the light or the darkness started to change. Through my eyelids I saw how everything around me rearranged itself in space. Each object seemed to exist only to create its distance from another object. The bottles on the red shelf, the hourglass, the bust with the title *"Espérance,"* the hammer that rested nearby on the windowsill, the silver sign with the word *"Réservé"* on it entered one by one into the play of distances.

Then the transparent rectangle became round and gradually grew wider and became a tube. I was at the end of the tube, near Dragoş, among the distances. I was calm again. In front of me the tube stretched like a giant spyglass, on whose edges something like a black but colorless circle was outlined. Actually, there was nothing there. And inside the circle a gentle bluish light floated, I don't know how to express it, a radiance where everything seemed bluish, into the far distance, endlessly. A rumble emanated from there, like the breathing of a giant whale. And there sat Zenobia on a heap of dry reeds, she was waiting for me, but I knew that she was on this side, at this end, which might have been the other end, and I didn't yet want to slip into the bluishness of the tube. "I'm behaving," I said to her, and both of us smiled.

I felt how the endless abyss tried to suck me in, but I managed to resist. Near my forehead Dragoş slept softly and motionlessly. I saw how his eyelashes grew longer and fluttered in the waves of light.

"Perhaps we are seeing each other for the last time," I said to him, "maybe you don't even exist, but I still have time to say one word to you, only one, the last . . ."

I told him the word, I won't repeat it, maybe I don't know it anymore, I blew it into his nostrils. He jumped, he looked at me for a moment with only one eye, he seemed indifferent, maybe he didn't even exist. Then I whined like a baby who notices his wet diaper and said: "I have to go, it's getting late and Zenobia is waiting for me, who knows how long she's been waiting for me . . ."

Then I left, the sun cast a last red flame. On my way I saw nobody. I walked on the dam, keeping away from the holes in order not to twist my ankle. There were a few black and friendly boulders over there, they looked at me as if we were brothers. They seemed glad to find me among them again.

In front of the hollow, Zenobia was sitting quietly on a heap of dry reeds with her hands in her lap. Her hair had turned gray from waiting . . .